FIREWORKS FOR MY DRAGON BOSS

A COZY MONSTER ROMANCE

FAIRHAVEN FALLS

HONEY PHILLIPS

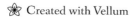 Created with Vellum

CHAPTER 1

*C*harlotte clutched the steering wheel as the tiny rental car jolted over another pothole, then checked her GPS for the tenth time. The screen continued to show nothing but the single white line of the road in an empty expanse of green.

"I know this is the right address," she muttered as she rounded a corner and had to swerve to avoid an overgrown bush. All evidence to the contrary.

The address had been buried in a very old contract. All of the newer contracts only used a PO box, but she'd dug through the files until she found an actual address—one that she could visit in person.

Something skittered across the road in front of her, and she slammed on her brakes, her heart threatening to jump out of her chest before she realized it was just a rabbit. On the rare occasions she had to drive in Manhattan she was used to dodging pedestrians and kamikaze bicycle delivery people, not animals. Right now she'd much rather have been surrounded by crowds and buildings than this narrow track through a forest beginning to turn orange and gold.

At least it's paved. Mostly.

The pavement didn't help when the trees on the right side of the road suddenly opened up to reveal a steep drop down the mountainside. The only barrier along the edge of the drop-off was a low strip of rusty metal, and her stomach churned. She'd never been good with heights.

She crept all the way to the left side of the narrow road, praying that no one would appear from the other direction, gritted her teeth, and kept going. This time, it was almost a relief when the wall of trees closed back around her.

Ten harrowing minutes later, the road finally stopped climbing, and a few minutes after that, it came to an abrupt end in a wide paved forecourt. A long four-car garage with sleek metal and frosted glass garage doors was placed to one side, while a striking contemporary house stood directly in front of her. Two massive stacked stone walls flanked an even taller central section sheathed in dark wooden panels and topped by an angled cantilever roof. Except for a tall, narrow section of glass next to the massive door, the facade was absolutely featureless.

So this was Nakor Earlsworth's house. It wasn't what she had expected. The novels written by Bird Publishing's highest selling—and most reclusive—author combined extensive historical details with the search for lost treasure by the swashbuckling hero. She had envisioned something more like a sprawling old house packed with artifacts instead of this minimalist modern design.

But the appearance of the house was irrelevant—the male hopefully lurking inside was the focus of her trip.

She pulled to one side, careful not to block any of the garage doors, and turned off the car. As she did, the engine made an odd gurgling noise and she gave it a worried look. After two delayed flights and a missed connection, the only rental car agency still open at the airport was Bob's Rental Cars and Boats —apparently because Bob had been in the process of returning his fishing boat to the lot. She'd carefully avoided asking why anyone would want to rent a boat at an airport and picked out the newest of the five cars he had on the lot.

Crossing her fingers, she gave the dashboard a hopeful pat, then stepped out of the car and looked around. Everything about the place whispered money, but absolutely nothing about it said welcome. No bushes, let alone flowers, softened the facade. The only greenery was a thin strip of manicured moss separating the paved stone of the entry porch from the paved stone of the parking area.

Under other circumstances, she would have turned around and left, but it wasn't an option. And given how difficult it had been to locate the address, let alone the house, she hadn't exactly expected an enthusiastic reception.

She straightened her jacket, hoping she presented the correct balance of professional and friendly, pushed her glasses up her nose and strode as confidently as she could across the paved court. As she did, she noticed that the slate tiles covering the surface had been arranged to create a series of large concentric circles. *A landing pad*, she thought, and shivered.

Because Nakor was not only rich, reclusive, and notoriously rude, he was also a dragon—an Other, one of the creatures of myth and legend who shared the Earth with humans. *He's just another author*, she told herself firmly as she arrived at the enormous front door and reached for the bell.

Except there was no bell. No button to press, no chain to pull, no knocker. No way to announce her presence.

Dammit. She took a deep breath and knocked on the heavy wooden slab. Three firm knocks that showed absolutely no hint of nerves. She hoped.

The knocks landed with a dull thud and she held her breath, waiting for some hint of movement inside.

Nothing.

She tried again, trying to knock louder this time, but only succeeded in bruising her knuckles. Still no response.

Maybe he isn't here?

It seemed unlikely. Given his reclusive lifestyle, she doubted he was off jaunting around town. Cradling her sore knuckles, she tried to peer through the narrow strip of glass next to the door. The glass was translucent, and all she could see was a bright blur from what might be a distant window.

She cupped her hands around her face, trying to make out more details.

"Mr. Earlsworth? My name is Charlotte Hudson. I'm here from Bird Publishing."

As she waited hopefully, a dark figure suddenly crossed in front of the light. A very large dark figure. Her heart skipped a beat as she tried to make out the details, but nothing moved. She took a deep breath and tried again.

"Mr. Earlsworth? I'm here on behalf of your publisher."

Nothing.

Dammit, this was ridiculous. She knew he was inside, and he clearly knew she was at the front door, but he was going to ignore her anyway? God, she wished she could just throw up her hands and walk away, but she couldn't. Bird Publishing had recently acquired the small publishing company she'd worked for since she graduated college, and the layoffs had been coming thick and fast.

She knew her job was on the line—which was why she'd volunteered to fly to the wilds of North Carolina and face Nakor once she'd located his address. The thought of losing her job made her stomach twist nervously. She had to get this asshole to talk to her, but how?

He wouldn't be the first difficult author she'd had to handle, but she'd never run into one who wouldn't even speak to her before. Usually a calm, sympathetic ear was all they really wanted. It would be rather difficult to project understanding and empathy through a closed door.

Maybe there's another window. Maybe if he could see her face, he'd realize she didn't represent a threat. Or be won over by my feminine charms, she thought, then rolled her eyes. She didn't have the personality—or the looks for that matter—to seduce him into listening to her. But at least she'd be harder to ignore if he could see her directly.

Something rustled in the trees to one side of the cleared area, and her heart skipped another beat. A small animal? Or something larger, like a bear or a mountain lion? Did they have mountain lions in these mountains?

I am so out of my depth here.

But she didn't have a choice, so she lifted her chin and began to walk briskly along the house, searching for another entrance.

Her sensible heels tapped firmly against the slate tiles. As she passed by the garage, she realized that there was light seeping through the frosted windows at the bottom edge. She paused for a moment before reluctantly deciding that breaking into his garage would probably be taking things too far.

The wall of vegetation next to the garage had been trimmed into a thick, precise hedge, and she quickly realized there was no way for her to make her way through it. The other side of the parking area looked more open, but as she drew closer, she realized it was because the mountainside dropped away immediately behind the thin row of trees. Her throat went dry as she very cautiously backed away from the edge.

Now what? If this had been Manhattan she would have simply headed out to find a café and returned again later, but the closest coffee shop was in Fairhaven Falls—and the small town was at the bottom of the long, narrow mountain road.

She sighed, then returned to the front porch and knocked again, on the window this time.

"Mr. Earlsworth? Don't you think you're being rather childish about this?" *Oops.* That came out a little more honestly than she'd intended. "I'm here to help you," she added quickly.

There was a muffled thud from the other side of the door, then a loud click. *That sounded like a lock,* she thought as her pulse quickened. She drew a deep breath as the heavy door swung silently open.

And then she looked up... and up.

Her heart started to pound. She'd seen Others before—a were-wolf in a suit and tie hurrying off to Wall Street or a dryad amidst the trees in Central Park—but in the city they were far outnumbered by humans. Instead, the Others tended to prefer small towns like Fairhaven Falls. She'd known that, of course, and she'd barely even blinked when her innkeeper introduced her to her huge troll fiancé. But the big male with the friendly smile sitting behind the desk hadn't prepared her for being this close to an angry dragon.

Angry—and shockingly handsome, his sharp, chiseled features accented by the twin horns rising from each temple beneath thick dark hair with burnished gold highlights. He was wearing tailored black pants and a white dress shirt, but his shirt was open, revealing a wide expanse of heavily muscled flesh covered with shimmering golden skin.

He was also shockingly large, easily close to seven feet tall, even without the tips of his wings reaching another foot over his head. *Wings!* She'd known about those too, but it wasn't the same as seeing the huge golden membranes in person. Nor was she prepared for the heat radiating from that very large body, even with several feet between them.

But neither his height nor his warmth nor his impressive physique was the most intimidating thing about him. It was the almost incandescent rage beneath the mask of arrogant disdain.

"Childish?" he demanded. "Is that what you called me?"

The deep rumble of his voice vibrated through her, and she automatically found herself ducking her head as she desperately tried to come up with an explanation. A slender line of smoke trickled from one nostril as he waited impatiently.

Deciding to treat it as a rhetorical question, she forced a sympathetic smile to her face and raised her chin.

"Mr. Earlsworth, I'm sure you know that you are... behind on your contractual obligations. Bird is very anxious to obtain that manuscript. We understand that sometimes difficulties can arise that create unexpected delays. I'm simply here in order to help with any... obstacles that may be in your way."

Dark eyebrows drew together as he looked down at her with glittering amber eyes. "Did I invite you?"

"Well, umm, no."

"No." More smoke wafted from his nostrils and she had a brief, horrified vision of becoming a barbecued kebab.

"Your assistance is neither welcome nor necessary," he snapped. "Now leave."

The door slammed in her face, and she blinked, looking down at her suddenly trembling hands. This was bad. Very, very bad.

Now what was she going to do?

CHAPTER 2

*P*acing restlessly back and forth across his living room, his tail lashing behind him, Nakor glared in the direction of his front door.

The annoying female should have left by now, but she was still there, still staring up at his house. He could see her through the security cameras as she gazed around his property as if in search of answers, twisting her fingers together nervously. She seemed ridiculously small, even for a human, but he had to give her a tiny bit of credit for not screaming and running as soon as he opened the door.

The wide grey eyes that had peered up at him from behind those black frames were clearly terrified, but she hadn't backed down. She'd barely even flinched when he breathed smoke at her, although her lips had formed a rather appealing pink circle. *Not a relevant thought,* he decided and headed for his study.

Unfortunately, hiding away—*working*—in his study didn't remove her from his thoughts, especially since any other ideas were sadly absent. He looked down at the quill pen in his hand, then cast it aside in disgust. He'd never resorted to such methods before—he'd always written on a computer the way God had intended. But his complete inability to produce new words had driven him to such desperate attempts to try and trick his brain into working again.

And it was all that fucking publishing company's fault. He'd been just fine without them and their contracts and their deadlines. Contracts he should just walk away from. It wasn't as if he needed the money. He had millions in his hoards—his bank accounts, he corrected automatically. He was a modern dragon, and modern dragons didn't have hoards.

But it wasn't the money that prevented him from walking away. It was the fact that he had given his word—a word he now seemed incapable of fulfilling.

He scowled and flicked on the security monitor again. Yes, she was still there, pacing back and forth and giving the surrounding woods suspicious looks. Since his publisher was located in New York, she was undoubtedly a city girl and not used to nature. Should he tell her that no dangerous wildlife would get within a mile of his territory?

No. The possibility of vicious animals would be one more incentive to make her leave.

Except she didn't leave. He made himself a perfectly brewed espresso using his custom picked beans and carried it out to the balcony, seeking the usual peace he found under the open sky, but the knowledge of her presence even tainted his coffee. He returned to his study and picked up a book, but he couldn't lose himself in the words. He would have gone to his garage to work on one of his cars, but the knowledge she would be on the other side of the glass dissuaded him. Not even spending time with his personal hoard—*collection*—soothed him.

When she knocked again, he stalked to the front door and flung it open, only to stop short when he realized she was standing directly in front of the door, her face almost colliding with his ribs. He took a hasty step back as a hint of her tantalizing floral scent reached him.

"What now?" he demanded.

"I'm sorry to disturb you, Mr. Earlsworth, but I was wondering if I could get a cup of tea?"

She spoke rapidly, her cheeks flushed, but the determined tilt of her chin didn't falter.

"Tea?"

"Yes, please."

"You interrupted me to ask for a cup of tea?"

The tip of her small pink tongue slid out to wet her lower lip. "It was a long drive up the mountain, and I forgot my water bottle."

He crossed his arms and did his best to ignore the way her eyes followed the gesture.

"Then you should start back down now."

"I'm not leaving until you talk to me. Maybe over a cup of tea?" she added hopefully.

Damn, she was persistent. He rather admired her tenacity—not that he had any intention of admitting it.

"Why would I possibly offer you a cup of tea?"

"Because that's what civilized people do? And I'm thirsty."

Now she was accusing him of being uncivilized? Dragons had been civilized long before these primitive humans.

"Civilized?" he asked coldly. "Civilized people do not show up uninvited at a private residence and then demand tea. You are far from civilized, human."

"Don't be rude. My name is Charlotte, not human. You wouldn't like it if I just called you dragon."

The flush of anger on her cheeks was unexpectedly appealing—and he reluctantly admitted that she had a point.

"Very well, Charlotte."

"Thank you. Now are you going to give me some tea or not?"

The combination of defiance and hope in those big grey eyes tugged at him, but he had no intention of falling for such blatant emotional manipulation.

"Fine," he growled.

"Thank you," she said quickly and hurried inside, her small body almost brushing against his in her haste.

Did she think he was going to slam the door in her face? *Perhaps that would have been the wiser choice*, he thought with a silent groan, as his body reacted to that brief closeness. It had obviously been far too long since he'd been around a female if he was responding to this tiny human.

Keeping a safe distance away from her beguiling scent, he led her into his kitchen and stopped at one end of the long marble-topped island. She came to an abrupt halt on the other side, and her eyes widened as she looked around, taking in the high-end European cabinetry and expensive appliances. He waited expectantly for her admiration, but she barely seemed to notice. Instead, she focused on the wall of windows that lined one side of the kitchen, showcasing a breathtaking view of the mountains and valleys falling away to the distant horizon.

"Wow," she said finally.

At least this time she appeared satisfactorily impressed. Appeased by her appreciation, he opened his lacquered Chinese tea cabinet and considered the options.

"Would you prefer black, green, or white tea?"

"White tea? I've never heard of that."

"I have an excellent Jinggu Silver Needle."

Not that he expected her to have the palate to enjoy it, but he would never dishonor his home by offering an inferior version, even if such a thing had ever crossed his threshold.

"Umm... yes, please."

Watching her out of the corner of his eye, he opened his tea chest and pulled out the correct canister. Regrettably, she didn't seem to appreciate the variety of rare blends, and he did his best not to scowl as he retrieved a glass teapot and set the water to heat to the correct temperature. It was only after he chose two appropriate cups that he realized that she was watching him rather than his preparations.

"Do I meet with your approval?"

He intended the question sarcastically, but he immediately regretted asking it. Her approval meant nothing to him after all.

"Yes... I mean, no... I mean..." She cleared her throat. "I've never been around a dragon before."

He fought back the instinct to preen. He was an exceptional specimen for her first encounter.

"Our physical forms are very different."

"Yes," she murmured as her eyes drifted across his chest, and more of the enchanting pink covered her cheeks.

His scales prickled with a sudden wariness. He found that shy speculation far too appealing.

"Dragon anatomy is far superior to human anatomy," he said firmly.

"Really?"

Despite the annoying doubt in her voice, he saw the brief flick of her eyes down over his body, and once again his body threatened to respond.

"Without a doubt."

Her eyes flashed back up to his, then her cheeks turned even pinker before she cleared her throat and looked away again.

"May I sit?"

The rituals of polite society allowed him no choice—and he was uneasily aware that he should have already offered her a seat. Biting back an apology, he pulled a stool away from the island and presented it to her.

With another shy smile she tried to climb up on it, but it had been designed for someone of his size. She was so ridiculously small that she had a hard time finding her balance. He sighed and put his hands on her waist to lift her onto the seat. As soon as he touched her, he knew it was a mistake.

CHAPTER 3

*T*he sweet, soft curve of Charlotte's waist beneath Nakor's hands sent an unwanted wave of arousal coursing through his body. The primitive side he usually kept so tightly reined roared to life—urging him to lift her higher, to stretch her out on the counter in front of him and feast on that delectable little body.

What the fuck is wrong with me? The fact that he should even be considering such a thing—with a human—stoked the fire of his anger. Ignoring the flare of heat, he set her precisely on top of the stool, careful to keep his touch impersonal, and quickly retreated—*returned*—to the other side of the counter as she gave a startled squeak.

The hunter in him wanted to pursue more of those delightful sounds, but he concentrated on preparing the tea instead, aware that her wide grey eyes followed every movement.

"That looks awfully complicated. You really don't have to go to this much trouble. You could just microwave some hot water and pop a tea bag into it."

He gave her an outraged glare.

"There are no tea bags in this house." Was she smiling at him? Ignoring her impertinence, he continued his lecture. "Brewing tea properly may be less convenient, but it allows one to fully appreciate the full spectrum of the beverage. To understand the nuances. To know how long to allow the leaves to infuse in order to achieve the perfect flavor."

Humans rarely appreciated the subtleties of life that made it worth living.

"How interesting," she murmured politely, but he still had a suspicion that she was laughing at him.

"What are you really doing here?" he demanded.

She bit her lip at the sudden change of subject, but looked him directly in the eye.

"I told you, I'm here because of the deadline."

He didn't respond, and she finally sighed and shot him a disgruntled look.

"You do know the manuscript is late, don't you? Very late."

He refused to discuss it, despite the unwelcome feeling of guilt.

"And why is that your concern, Ms. Hudson?"

"Charlotte. Please call me Charlotte. It's my concern because my boss sent me here to talk to you since you aren't answering calls. Or emails. Or letters." She hesitated, then added softly, "And because I'm a fan."

18

His pride wanted to believe her, but it wouldn't be the first time a human had lied to him.

"You truly enjoy my books?" he asked skeptically.

The pretty pink touched her cheeks again.

"Of course I do. You have an amazing grasp of language and a fascinating way of conveying the historical information behind the treasures. Your books feel so real—as if I'm there with Griff on his adventures." She paused as her color deepened. "I'm sure you hear that kind of thing all the time and that's not why I'm here. I really do want to help. I will do everything I can to resolve any... conflicts you have that are preventing you from finishing the book."

She seemed so sincere that he almost considered confiding in her. Instead, he just shook his head.

"There is nothing you can do."

She smiled up at him. "Maybe you just need to be willing to accept help."

It was such a nonsensical statement that he wasn't sure whether he wanted to laugh or growl. Instead, he turned his attention back to the tea. She leaned forward to watch as he gently spooned the silver needle buds into the glass pot. He poured the hot water over them, making sure that each bud was covered, then stood back to wait.

Once the tea reached the perfect color and aroma, he carefully poured it into the waiting cups. He had chosen cream-colored porcelain with a crackled orange glaze to reflect the season. He passed one of the cups to her and watched as she lifted it to her nose and sniffed.

"Mmm," she whispered and her lips curved into a smile. "This smells amazing."

Once again, her appreciation satisfied him.

"Indeed. The taste is just as sublime. Take a small sip and swirl it over your tongue to appreciate the nuances."

"Okay."

She lifted the cup to her mouth, her eyelids fluttering closed as she took a cautious sip. He watched in fascination as a blissful expression spread across her face and she hummed approvingly. Did she always respond so sensually to physical pleasure?

Pushing aside the unwelcome curiosity, he settled down on the opposite side of the counter. The two of them sipped in silence and an odd peace filled the sunlit kitchen. For a moment he could almost forget why she was here.

"This was wonderful," she said with a sigh as she put the empty cup down. "Thank you."

Her gratitude pleased him, and when she licked the last drop from her lips, he felt another stirring of arousal. How had this tiny human female managed to capture his attention? He didn't know and he didn't like it, but he still found himself reluctant to just demand that she leave.

As if anticipating him, she folded both hands neatly on the counter and gave him a penetrating look.

"Now, why don't you tell me what's really going on?"

"Nothing," he said immediately, hoping he didn't sound as defensive as he felt.

"You've never missed a deadline before this book, but you're six months past the date when you were supposed to submit it. If you don't turn in a completed draft soon, the company could decide to take legal action."

The implied threat angered him, and he glared at her.

"They are welcome to try."

An annoyingly adorable frown drew her small brows together. "Don't you care? You may have a fortune in gold buried somewhere, but even a dragon should know that lawsuits cost money. Lawyers aren't cheap."

She dared to mention his hoard—*bank account?* The little vixen was trying to goad him into anger, but he refused to take the bait.

"I know. I may even offer a substantial bonus to any lawyer who will take the case."

"Don't you think that's rather petty?"

"And invading my home is not?"

She flinched at the question, but immediately lifted her chin again.

"I came here to help you."

"Do I appear to need any assistance?"

"Mr. Earlsworth—Nakor—please. We're on the same side here. You want to release your book. Bird wants to publish it. No one really wants the time and expense of a lawsuit. All I want to do is find a way to help you move forward."

"If you wish to help, then leave and forget about this nonsense."

"I can't."

For the first time, he saw something more than determination in her face—a flash of fear—and it aroused his curiosity.

"Why not?"

"Because my job depends on it."

He believed her. For a moment he was tempted to relent, but then he reminded himself that humans were not to be trusted. And even if he wanted to comply, he couldn't force the words on to the page.

"That is unfortunate," he said coldly.

She made a choked sound, then sighed. "Can't you at least give me some hint as to how much longer it might take? You've released enough books to know all the tasks that have to be scheduled around the launch date."

"My creative process is no one else's business."

"It's your publisher's business!"

She glared at him in exasperation, and he could see that she was beginning to lose her temper. It would have been amusing —but her face suddenly changed. Her lips pursed in a look that was somehow both mutinous and adorable, and it made his cock press painfully against his sheath.

"You have writer's block, don't you?" she said softly.

"Of course not."

She ignored his denial, reaching over to give his hand a sympathetic pat. He certainly did not need her sympathy, nor did he want his unruly body to respond to those small soft fingers covering his hand.

"There's nothing to be ashamed of," she said quickly. "It can happen to anyone."

"I don't have writer's block!"

He might as well not have spoken since she clearly wasn't listening.

"I know I can help you overcome it," she said enthusiastically. "I've studied some methods that can help."

The combination of frustration, anger, lust, and what he refused to admit was fear spurred him into a terrible decision.

"I don't have writer's block," he repeated, trying to control his anger. "And what I need is an assistant."

CHAPTER 4

*C*harlotte blinked across at Nakor, thinking she must have misheard him. "An assistant?"

"Yes, an assistant. I am... behind on my research. If you can gather the information I need, then I *may* be able to commit to a firm date."

Did he really mean it? She hadn't expected the arrogant male to actually admit he needed help. Then again, she hadn't really even expected that he would let her into his house. Her request for tea had been a long shot at best, but in one of his files a former editor had mentioned his interest in tea—and it had worked.

"Of course," she said at once. "I'll do whatever I can to help you get back on track before I leave."

"Leave?"

"My flight back to New York is scheduled for Thursday."

He frowned, then nodded.

"Perhaps that is just as well. Shall we begin?"

"Yes, of course!"

She did her best to conceal her excitement. After all, she hadn't exactly won the argument about him turning in his manuscript. But the fact that he'd asked for help was a huge win, and she wasn't about to mess things up now.

"Come with me," he ordered.

She slid gracelessly off the oversized barstool and followed him from the kitchen into an equally impressive living room with expensive grey leather couches. The walls were a warm, buttery gold, a dramatic contrast to the subtle colors of the slate tile floor, and a massive fireplace occupied most of an inside wall. The two exterior walls were composed entirely of glass, jutting out over the cliff to take advantage of another stunning view. She gave them an admiring glance, but she had no intention of getting any closer.

He strode over to a heavy wooden door set in the wall next to the fireplace, swinging it open to reveal a large study with floor-to-ceiling shelves lining three walls. A comfortable chair sat in front of a large picture window on the fourth wall, while a sleek contemporary desk dominated the rear of the room. A luxurious white carpet covered the center of the tile floor.

"What kind of research do you need me to do?" she asked curiously.

He stalked across the room to his desk, then waited for her to join him. As she did, she was once again conscious of his size and the heat emanating from his body, and a reluctant flicker of arousal teased her nipples into stiff little points. She did her best to ignore it and concentrate on his words as she frowned down at his desk.

"You know this book is based on a search for ancient Persian treasures, right? I need more information on their legends in order to incorporate them."

"I see. How do you usually do your research?"

His books always contained a huge amount of historical information that he somehow managed to make both interesting and accessible.

"I have... connections with a variety of academic sources, and much of it takes place online. However, I also have some physical reference materials that have not yet been digitized."

"And you have them here?"

He pointed to a section of shelving behind the desk.

"These are the ones I have obtained for this book."

She ran a tentative hand over the collection, many of them long out of print, and smiled, already anticipating the search.

"Is there something specific you need me to look for?"

"The legends say that the god Ahriman was imprisoned deep below the earth. Griff's search for the treasure takes him on a similar journey to a place where he will face the ultimate challenge and test his courage and strength against the demon lord."

He frowned again, and she couldn't help thinking that his horns gave him a slightly demonic appearance as well. *A very sexy demon.*

"Is something wrong?" she asked, doing her best to ignore the unwanted thought.

"You will need a workspace." Something crossed his face that she couldn't read. "Wait here. Don't touch anything."

She rolled her eyes and very deliberately picked up one of the books he had indicated as soon as he left the room. After all, she wasn't going to be able to do much research unless she could read them. She half-expected him to return and carry her off to some tiny cubicle to work. Instead, he returned with another chair—one he placed at the desk, right next to his. *Oh.*

That meant they would be working a lot closer than she'd anticipated, but then again, it was an enormous desk.

He glanced over at her, his gaze immediately dropping to the book in her hands. For a moment he stiffened, but then a startlingly attractive smile suddenly washed over his face. *Wow.* He was good-looking enough when he was being cold and arrogant—she wasn't sure she could handle that smile on top of it.

"I see you're eager to get started," he said dryly.

"Anything to help, remember?" she asked sweetly, and his smile flashed again before he shook his head and turned to his own work.

The rest of the day passed with surprising speed. She had always enjoyed research, and the variations of the legends that she uncovered were fascinating. As she recorded her notes in the laptop he'd provided for her, she couldn't help noticing that his original coldness had returned. He only spoke to her twice —once to ask if she wanted anything to eat, which she declined, and once to ask her if she wanted another cup of tea, which she gratefully accepted.

By the time the sun dipped towards the horizon, she was tired and hungry and her neck ached from bending over the keyboard. She rose and stretched, then realized he was watching her. She'd discarded her jacket during the afternoon and the silk shell she'd been wearing underneath it suddenly seemed far too thin.

"I'm going to leave now because I don't want to drive down the mountain in the dark. If you don't mind me taking some of these with me, I can keep working in my room at the inn."

"I would prefer they remained here. But come back early tomorrow."

"I think you meant to say *please* come back early."

His amber eyes glittered, but she refused to back down, and eventually he inclined his head slightly.

"Very well. Please come back early."

"Thank you. I'll see you tomorrow."

Triumph carried her all the way out of the house and over to the rental car. There was a message from her boss on her phone, but she decided to wait until she was back at the inn to tackle it. She'd use the drive to decide on the best way of presenting the day's events. Already considering options, she turned the key.

Nothing happened.

She tried again, but the engine didn't even turn over. She looked from the car to the shadows already creeping across the road down the mountain, and then she sighed and headed back to the house.

CHAPTER 5

amn. Nakor swore under his breath as Charlotte left. The afternoon had not gone as he planned. He'd regretted the foolish impulse to ask her to assist him as soon as the words had come out of his mouth, but he had too much pride to retract them.

He'd hoped that she would get bored or restless or that she would do a terrible job and he would have an excuse to demand that she leave. Instead, she'd actually seemed to enjoy the research, and the notes she'd added to the shared drive were clear and thorough, if occasionally a little fanciful. *As if she were already imagining the hero pursuing his quest based on her research*, he thought, then scowled.

Her ability to produce words, even if they were only research notes, had made him that much more conscious of his own inability, which annoyed him. The fact that he'd also been far too conscious of her hadn't helped. What on earth had possessed him to share the desk with her?

He found himself watching out of the corner of his eye as the silk covering her small breasts rose and fell with each breath. Or the way she chewed thoughtfully on her pen when she was reading, her pretty lips pursed around the slender shaft. Of the delicate fragrance of her hair when she pushed it over her shoulder and out of her way. How many times had he considered burying his fingers in those soft strands and giving her something much more interesting to put in her mouth?

He swore again as his cock jerked. He thought of trying to relieve the tension—and there was that knock again. He certainly did *not* hurry to the door to see what she wanted.

As soon as he opened it, she gave him an anxious look, her hands twisting together again.

"I'm really sorry to bother you, but my car won't start. It made this weird gurgling noise earlier, and now when I turn the key nothing happens."

Her eyes were wide and hopeful behind her glasses, and he gave into another foolish impulse.

"Do you want me to fly you back to town?"

His cock throbbed at the thought, already imagining her small body locked against his as they soared through the sky. She obviously did not share his enthusiasm. Her eyes widened as she backed away a step.

"N-no, that's all right. I just thought maybe you had a car. Never mind. I can always walk."

"In the dark?" he asked skeptically. He could easily envision her trying to pick her way down the road in the dark, tripping and falling down the mountain. Dammit, she was going to hurt herself.

"All right," he sighed. "I'll take you in one of my cars."

"Oh, thank you." Her radiant smile did something strange and unwanted to his insides. "I didn't think I'd be able to get a tow truck up here in the dark."

He should have told her no, but it was almost dark already. He refused to admit that the idea of driving her back to town appealed to him.

"Fine. I'll be with you in a minute."

He stalked to the garage and, after a brief hesitation, chose his mint condition '55 Chevy truck. It was the safest vehicle for her to ride in—even if it did have a manual transmission.

He pulled out, then held the door open as she hurried over to join him. Once again he found himself lifting her, this time onto the high bench seat, but he managed to keep his face impassive as he closed the door behind her. She smiled at him as he came around to join her, running a hand over the pristine red leather.

"This truck is amazing. I've never seen one in such good condition."

He nodded, appeased by her appreciation.

"It's a classic vehicle."

"I'll say. I had a boyfriend in high school with one of these. The sides were dented, the leather was torn, and it had more rust than paint, but it still kept going."

His hands tightened on the wheel at the mention of another male.

"I would never allow one of my vehicles to remain in that condition."

She surprised him by laughing.

"Somehow I don't doubt that. Thanks again for doing this. I'm sorry if I disturbed your work."

"I had finished for the evening," he said truthfully.

She made an agreeable noise, then lapsed into silence as she looked out over the passing scenery. A few minutes later, she shivered.

"Are you cold?" he asked.

"Not really. I'm just not used to the mountain air."

The breeze wafting through the open window had been a pleasant coolness against his heated skin, but she looked so small and fragile that he quickly closed his window, then reached down to adjust the heater. He had never actually used it before, although of course he'd made sure it was working perfectly. As the blowers came on, the blast of hot air blew directly on her thighs, and he caught a brief glimpse of creamy flesh before she quickly pulled her legs together.

"Oh my God," she whispered, and her voice was shaky.

"Do you want me to turn the heat back off?"

"No. It just surprised me."

He didn't argue, even though he noticed that she kept her knees together for the remainder of the drive. He also caught the faint sweetness of her arousal every time the warm air wafted through the cabin of the truck. Would she react as delightfully if he were to bathe her in the heat of his breath? Or perhaps she would prefer his hands and his tongue and his... He abruptly cut off the thought and tried to concentrate on the drive.

Despite her attempts to hide it, the scent of her arousal only grew stronger, and he found himself driving faster. By the time they reached the inn, his entire body was tense with arousal and he could barely restrain himself.

"I'll see you in the morning," she said brightly as she turned to thank him.

"Early," he snapped, then forced himself to add, "please."

"Okay. And thanks again for the ride."

She smiled and began to swing her legs out of the cab, but he reached across the seat and stopped her. Her sweet scent surrounded him, teasing him and sending more blood surging to his already aching cock.

"Let me lift you out."

"Oh, umm... all right."

She gave him an expectant look when he came to the open door of the truck and raised her arms, clearly expecting him to put his hands on her waist again. Instead, he hooked one hand under her bottom and lifted her directly up against him. Her arms went around his neck, her eyes widening and her lips parting as he brought her closer and the thick bulge in his pants pressed against the juncture of her thighs.

"Nakor," she whispered, her face inches away from his, then leaned forward and covered his mouth with hers.

His head reeled as her soft lips pressed against his, already parted in invitation. He took immediate advantage, plunging his tongue into the delicious depths of her mouth. She whimpered as his tongue teased hers, and his hips bucked, mimicking the kiss and grinding his cock between her spread thighs. She arched towards him, her stiff nipples like burning brands against his chest as she moaned into his mouth. Her hands tightened on his shoulders, holding him close as she gave him everything he demanded.

Her tiny tongue circled around his before she nipped at his lower lip, then soothed the small sting with the tip of her tongue. *Fuck*, she tasted sweet. His cock grew impossibly harder, trying to breach the layers of clothing between their bodies. Her sweet little pussy would be so hot and tight around his cock as he plunged into her...

He growled as he yanked away from her, suddenly remembering where they were. She stumbled and nearly fell without his support, and he cursed as he steadied her. Her eyes were dazed as she looked up at him, but the heat he'd seen in them had been replaced by confusion and anxiety.

"Nakor," she whispered in an apologetic tone. "I—I didn't—"

"Good night," he said firmly as he saw Alison, the innkeeper, watching them from the porch of the inn.

He started to return to the truck, then swore and turned back.

"Can you drive a stick shift?"

She still looked dazed, her mouth pink and swollen, but she nodded.

"Here." He tossed her the keys. "You'll need a way up the mountain in the morning."

"But..."

He didn't wait to hear the rest, leaping into the sky before he did something stupid like pick her up and carry her back to his cave. No, his *house*. Neither, dammit. He wasn't carrying her anywhere.

He circled higher, still fighting the urge to return, then drifted over the town on the evening breeze, seeking a measure of peace in the familiar sights. He rarely went into town any more, but he frequently observed it from the air. The lights were coming on in the town square and the River Café was already full of diners. They spilled out onto the deck despite the coolness of the autumn evening, and he watched a pink-haired pixie teasing an ogre three times her size.

The water next to Sam's island rippled as the kraken slipped quietly into the water and he sketched a silent salute. Another male who preferred to be on his own. And thinking of males who preferred to be on their own... He circled again, then flew down to land outside a house on the edge of town.

Trogar was sitting on his front porch, also looking out over the town.

"Nakor," the orc acknowledged. "Want a beer?"

"I don't suppose you have any craft beers?"

Trogar didn't bother to reply, just tossed a can of PBR over to him. He sighed, drank half of it in one gulp, then scowled at his friend.

"Why do females make life so complicated?"

The orc arched a brow.

37

"Fortunately, I have no idea. I do know that by the time you start asking that, it's too fucking late."

"No, it's not," he said immediately. "It's just a temporary... aberration."

"What's an aberration?" Flora said cheerfully as she appeared out of the bushes.

He managed to conceal his reaction, but Trogar scowled at the tiny old woman in the sequined tracksuit.

"Dammit, Gran. Stop sneaking up on people."

"It's not my fault you pay so little attention to your senses. My generation can spot someone coming a mile away." She smirked at Nakor. "Your grandfather wasn't bad either. Why, I remember back in my courting days, he'd be swooping down to carry me off every time I left the house. But then my mate won me over with his huge co—"

"Gran!"

Flora grinned and thankfully stopped talking—but then she focused back on him, dark eyes twinkling.

"What aberration? It wouldn't be a certain pretty little female from the big city, would it?"

"No," he snapped.

He tossed the empty beer can into the trash barrel, extended his wings, then hesitated.

"Make sure she eats something, will you?"

Her eyes were entirely too knowing as she gave him an innocent smile.

"Of course, dear. With your compliments?"

Infuriating old woman. He growled and leaped into the air, but her laughter followed him.

CHAPTER 6

*C*harlotte stared after Nakor as he flew off into the sky and left her standing by the truck, still reeling from the kiss.

Kiss? That hadn't just been a kiss. It had been a possession. A claiming. A promise of what would happen if she didn't stop him.

Stop him? Who was she kidding? She'd been seconds away from wrapping herself around him and begging for more when he pushed her away from him.

It's just as well, she told herself as firmly as possible. She was supposed to be here to work. To work. *Oh, God.* She groaned and headed over to the porch on still not entirely steady legs.

"I see you found Nakor's house," Alison said, smiling at her.

The pretty innkeeper had been the one to confirm her directions that morning. Was it only that morning? It felt like a lifetime ago.

"Will says he's very territorial, and it looks like he's right," the other woman added.

She knew she was blushing as she dropped into the seat next to Alison and groaned again.

"I don't know what happened. I didn't even think he liked me."

"I think you can set your mind at ease about that," Alison said dryly as she handed her a soft woven throw.

"You don't understand. The last thing I need is to get involved with one of our authors. Especially with my job hanging on by a thread."

"Is it that bad?"

There was nothing but friendly sympathy in the other woman's face, and she found herself recounting her woes.

"Worse. I love my job—or at least I did. I've never made much money, and I live in the tiniest studio apartment imaginable, but I really enjoyed being a part of getting people's books out into the world."

"I've lived in a lot of cities myself. I don't miss them," Alison said, smiling out into the gathering darkness as a few early leaves scurried across the neatly manicured lawn. "I love it here. Everyone's so nice." A tall, misty shape drifted across the lawn, and she laughed. "A little different maybe, but nice."

Charlotte decided she didn't want to ask.

"I never thought I wanted to live anywhere other than New York, but then our company was acquired twice in less than three years. I barely know anyone anymore and it's all spreadsheets and meetings."

"You can't say you don't know anyone now," the other woman teased. "Looks like you're getting to know Nakor extremely well."

"But I'm not supposed to get to know him like that," she wailed. "I'm only here for a few days, just to get him back on track."

"A few days?" Alison gave her a puzzled look. "But I thought Flora said you'd be here for at least—"

"There you both are." Flora suddenly appeared on the porch next to them, and both women jumped. "Where's your handsome mate, Alison?"

"Working on our house of course. He wants to have it done by the wedding."

"He will," the old lady said firmly. "I'm sure the weather will hold out."

"I bet it will," Alison muttered, then rose and stretched. "Now that you're here, I think I'll go take him home. Will you lock up?"

"Of course I will. Have fun! Don't do anything I wouldn't do."

"I doubt that eliminates much." Alison grinned affectionately as she bent down and kissed Flora's cheek, then disappeared back behind the inn.

Flora took her place, rocking in silence for a few minutes as the tiny lights lining the driveway popped on, and Charlotte gave her a curious look from under her lashes. Alison had told her that the tiny old lady was also an orc, but it seemed almost impossible.

"It's entirely possible," Flora said, her eyes closed. "I inherited one of my ancestor's genes. She was a fairy."

43

She flushed guiltily as the old lady turned and smiled at her.

"I'm sorry. I didn't mean to stare."

"You're not the first, and you won't be the last. Besides, I like confounding expectations."

She shrugged uncomfortably. "I'm afraid I've always been the conventional type."

"Don't be silly. You seem to be adapting to our town very well."

Despite the innocent tone, Charlotte was suddenly quite sure that Flora knew everything that had happened that day.

"Maybe, but it's just temporary," she said firmly. "I'm leaving Thursday."

"Oh, you never know what might happen." Flora waved an airy hand as she rose to her feet. "There might even be an early snowstorm. Although somehow I don't think that will be necessary."

Charlotte gave her a confused look as she stood as well, but managed a polite nod.

"Umm, okay."

"Are you going to be up much later, my dear? I'm going to lock up now, although you can always use your key if you need to go out."

"I have absolutely no interest in going out," she said with a tired sigh as they entered the inn. "I'm just going to grab a snack from the kitchen and go to bed. I have an early start tomorrow."

"You don't need to worry about finding a snack. There's a tray in your room already. Good night, dear."

Flora disappeared as rapidly as she'd appeared, leaving Charlotte staring after her in bemusement. Since she was really too tired to worry about it, she climbed the stairs to her room, sighing with pleasure as she walked in. The huge room was actually larger than her studio, and included high ceilings, tall windows, and beautiful old wood floors. The bedding, curtains, and three of the walls were white, but the wallpaper behind the bed was an oversized rose print and more pops of pink and red softened the white.

A tray on the table in front of the window contained a still steaming bowl of chicken soup, homemade bread, and a cookie as big as her fist. She ate eagerly, then carried her glass of wine into the bathroom to find the clawfoot tub already full of hot water, rose petals floating on the surface and perfuming the air.

"Magic," she whispered. It had to be, but it was such a warm, comfortable magic that the thought only made her smile.

After a long bath, she slept better than she had in ages and woke up full of determination. The sun wasn't even up, but she dressed quickly and quietly headed for the truck. Today was going to be different. No illicit passionate kisses, just business.

Her resolution lasted throughout the drive as she steered the truck cautiously up the mountain road. Fortunately, dawn had broken and she could clearly see the narrow track. She made it back to the house without incident and parked the truck neatly next to the garage.

"Business," she reminded herself firmly as she strode over to the door and knocked.

A resolution that disappeared as soon as the door opened to reveal a very wet, very angry, and almost naked dragon.

CHAPTER 7

*N*akor did not sleep well. His thoughts were haunted by the annoyingly tempting female. By the memory of her mouth opening beneath his, sweet and soft and unbearably delicious. By those slender curves molded against his body and the warmth of her sweet little cunt as she rocked against his cock.

He woke with his cock throbbing in his hand, spilling seed into the sheets, and he cursed viciously. What the fuck was wrong with him? She was just another human—a small, defenseless female—annoying and determined and incredibly beautiful.

Determined not to think about her anymore, he went and curled up with his hoard—in his *storage room*—but even the glitter of precious metals and the sparkle of jewels didn't distract him. Instead, he kept imagining her there with him, draped in his treasures, and by the time dawn broke he was tired, irritated, and his cock could have punched a hole in the steel walls of his storage room.

He detested giving in to physical limitations, but if he had any hope of making it through the day with his sanity intact, he didn't see any alternative but to take himself in hand. He adjusted the multiple jets of his elaborate shower and stepped under the hot water, his hand already grasping his cock.

He'd only managed two firm strokes, his spine already beginning to tingle, when he heard the knock on the door. With a roar, he grabbed the nearest towel, stomped into the foyer, and flung the door open.

"What do you want?"

Charlotte squeaked and backed up a step, her eyes wide as she looked up at him. Despite the anger boiling inside him, his cock immediately responded to that shy, speculative gaze.

"You told me to be here early," she said hesitantly as her eyes traveled down over his body, snagging on where his erection was tenting the towel. "Uh, I can go wait in the truck."

Fuck.

"Come inside and wait," he snapped, not caring how rude he sounded.

"Inside?"

She finally tore her gaze away from his cock and looked up at him, the pretty pink staining her cheeks.

"Inside," he repeated firmly, and slammed the door behind her as soon as she obeyed. "I'll be back in a minute."

He stalked off to his bedroom, his tail lashing behind him, and returned to the shower. With her scent still lingering in his lungs and the reality of her presence in his home, it only took another few strokes before he was shuddering out his release against the glass wall of the shower.

It didn't help.

He raked a comb through his hair and threw on a pair of dark pants. He didn't bother with a shirt. If she didn't want to see his bare chest, she didn't have to look at him. He almost yelled at her again when he found her using his imported Italian espresso maker, but she thrust a cup at him before he could speak.

The scent was better than he expected, with a perfect amount of crema on the top, and he took a cautious sip. The espresso was strong and smooth—perfect—and a tiny amount of tension began to leach from his body.

"How did you know how to make this?"

"It's not that complicated." She looked amused. "Besides, I worked as a barista while I was in college."

"You have some hidden talents," he muttered as he took another sip.

"Yours weren't very hidden," she said, then immediately blushed. "Sorry, sorry. sometimes my mouth gets ahead of my brain."

Her praise did not displease him, especially combined with the lingering relief of his climax and the truly excellent coffee.

"Why don't you make your own cup and meet me on the deck? We can discuss the work for the day."

It felt oddly like a truce, and the remaining tension in his body began to ease as he walked outside to admire the sunrise. She came out a moment later but instead of joining him at the railing, she remained pressed up against the wall of the house. Was she afraid to get close to him?

"What's wrong?" he demanded.

"I'm not good with heights."

"Don't be ridiculous. This deck is perfectly safe—I had it engineered to the highest standards."

Her chin came up. "I'm not being ridiculous and I'm perfectly comfortable over here."

"Well, I have no intention of yelling at you across the deck."

She didn't move, and neither did he. Finally he sighed and went to join her. She smiled up at him as she took a seat on one of the low couches arranged near the wall, but he didn't return the smile as he sat down next to her.

"Annoying female. The view is not as good from here."

"Thank you," she said softly. "And it's still a wonderful view."

She was looking at him as she spoke, and he couldn't help wondering if she was talking about the sunrise—or him. He found himself preening, and his tail slipped around her ankle as he settled back on the couch and resumed sipping his espresso.

"I thought I'd continue with my research today," she said when he didn't say anything else. "Is that what you wanted me to do?"

She was almost whispering, her voice so soft and so near that he could feel her breath stirring his skin. It would be so easy to take her in his arms, to plunder that soft mouth until she melted against him as she had the previous night. Until she surrendered to him, letting him do whatever he wanted with her, in whatever way he wanted... He caught himself as he almost growled in pleasure.

"That's fine. I have work to do as well."

"Good." She bit her lip and shot him a sideways glance. "Do you think you might be getting a better idea of your timeline?"

"After only one day's assistance? I don't think you're quite that good."

She lifted her chin again. Fuck, she was adorable—in an annoying kind of way.

"Perhaps not, but I'm good at organization. Maybe I should organize another assistant for you?"

"I don't want another assistant," he growled. "Now get to work."

"Yes, boss."

Despite the meek tone, he saw her hide a smile. Definitely annoying.

He made them both another espresso, then sent her off to his study while he went back out on the deck. What was he going to do? The work she was doing was extremely useful, and it would add character and depth to his book—if he ever managed to finish the damn thing. Not for the first time he wondered if he had chosen the wrong subject for this one. He'd begun to feel as if he were accompanying Griff on the descent into hell, but he hadn't managed to bring either one of them back to the surface yet.

The comfort of his hoard called to him, but as he started back through the living room, he heard the soft click of a keyboard. She'd left the door open, and he watched her frown thoughtfully, then push up those ridiculous glasses. He looked at the steps leading down to his storage room, then back at the pretty female working in his study. He sighed and went to join her.

CHAPTER 8

*C*harlotte did her best to concentrate on her research, but it wasn't easy. Nakor was a lot more distracting than she wanted to admit. She was supremely conscious of that big warm body next to her all day long. It didn't help that ever since that morning on the deck, his tail had a disconcerting tendency to slide over and curl around her ankle. Even more disconcertingly, she liked having it there. Most of the time it was rather like a giant ankle bracelet, but there were a couple of times when he was focused on something else and his tail would start to play.

The first time it slid up her calf, she jumped and he immediately yanked it away. The second time she managed to remain still, and it reached high enough to tease the sensitive back of her thighs before he pulled it away. Who would have thought that a tail—a tail!—could be so... tantalizing.

It's just because it's been such a long time, she told herself firmly. To a certain extent it was true—her already minimal dating life had suffered even more during the career chaos of the past few years—but deep down she knew it was more than that. She already admired him as an author, but meeting the real man—the real dragon—behind the books was completely different.

Yes, he was prickly and arrogant, but there was something else in his eyes—a loneliness that she recognized. He could also be unexpectedly kind, beneath that superior veneer. When she finished working at the end of the day, he walked her outside. Both the rental car and the truck were gone. Instead, a sleek little Porsche crossover waited.

"Where's the rental car?"

"I had it towed back. It wasn't safe."

She sighed, but she couldn't really argue with him.

"Umm, do you mind if I drive the truck again? I'll be very careful."

He frowned down at her.

"The truck is too tall for you. That's why I got this for you to use."

"You can't... I mean, I can't..."

"Unless you're going to insist on having me drive you back and forth each day, you don't have a choice. Is that what you want, sweetheart? For me to drive you?"

His voice had lowered to a silky purr, and she gulped as she remembered being pressed up against the truck with her legs around his waist. Heat pooled low in her stomach as she shook her head—not quite as convincingly as she would have liked.

"I'll borrow the car," she said shakily.

Was he disappointed? She couldn't tell. He bent his head towards her, but he didn't kiss her. He simply helped her into the car then stood back.

"Remember to come early tomorrow," he said gruffly as she drove away.

He was right about the Porsche being easy to drive, and she made it back to the inn without incident, her heart rate returning to normal only once she was safely parked.

That evening, Flora was nowhere in sight so she joined Alison and Will on the back deck for dinner. The food was simple but delicious—just as it had been the night before—and the conversation was fascinating. Alison and Will both regaled her with stories about the other inhabitants of the town. Their stories sounded more like fairy tales than reality, but the underlying current of warmth and affection was very real.

Then again, she was having dinner with an enormous troll with blue skin and green hair—her reality had definitely shifted. She couldn't help thinking that a big gold dragon would have completed the picture. What was he doing anyway, alone on his mountain?

"We're having a girls' night on Friday," Alison told her as the three of them carried the dishes back to the kitchen. "If you're still here, you should definitely come with us."

Will groaned and shook his head as he put his arm around his mate.

"If you do, don't take any drinks from my sister."

Alison laughed. "Nichola does tend to overestimate the human capacity for alcohol. I've taken to putting a spoonful of one of her specials into a glass of soda."

"She should be more careful," Will muttered.

"Oh, stop it. You know she means well—and she always makes sure we get home safely."

He grunted, obviously not convinced, and Charlotte smiled at her.

"It sounds like fun, but I have to fly back on Thursday."

Not that the prospect thrilled her.

Alison opened her mouth, shut it again, then sighed.

"I guess we'll wait and see. If you do need to stay, your room will be available."

"Why does everyone seem to think I'm going to stay?" She peered out the window at the clear, starlit sky. "Is there a storm coming that I should know about?"

"You never know." Will grinned at her, then picked Alison up and carried her towards the back door. "Come on, sugar. I want to show you what I've done today before we go home."

Charlotte followed them to the door, watching as they disappeared into the trees at the back of the property. They were so obviously happy together. She sighed, locked the door, then went up to her room.

She picked up her phone and hesitated, then sighed again and dialed the number for her editor. She'd chickened out and just sent an email the previous night, but she really should have talked to her.

"Oh. Hi, Charlotte. I'm glad you called. How's everything going?" Marjorie was clearly distracted, but that was fine with her.

"Really well. He seems to have been inspired, and we've been getting a lot of research done."

"That's right. You said you were helping him," Marjorie said absently. "Has he given you a new date yet?"

"He's not quite ready to commit to anything, but I think he'll be able to give me one before I leave on Thursday."

"Good." The other woman's voice suddenly sharpened as she focused on the call. "I don't have to tell you how critical the next Nakor Earlsworth book is to our fall lineup. You are going to make sure that happens, aren't you?"

The implied threat was quite clear.

"See that you do." The harsh words lingered for a moment, then Marjorie took a quick breath and started shuffling papers. "Can you join me for a virtual meeting at ten tomorrow?"

"I think it would be better to focus on Nakor," she said quickly.

"I suppose so. Call me as soon as you have that date."

The phone went dead before she could respond. At least Marjorie was willing to give her some more time to get an answer from Nakor—but was it going to be enough time? Even though he'd missed the original deadline, she truly believed that if he committed to a date in person, he would keep that date— now all she had to do was to get him to make the commitment.

Maybe I should try and apply some pressure. Just the thought made her shudder, and she couldn't see it going well. *Baby steps*, she told herself.

If only those baby steps weren't complicated by how much she was beginning to like him. And the attraction appeared to be mutual. He surely couldn't have kissed her the way he had the previous night if he wasn't interested—could he? And then there was that enormous erection that had been tenting his towel that morning. Was she wrong in thinking she might have had something to do with it? But perhaps he always woke up that way.

She squirmed at the thought of finding out, her nipples tightening into hard little points as she remembered that massive bulge. If only she were the kind of woman who would have just reached out and pushed the towel aside. What did his cock look like? As golden as the rest of his skin, or dark and swollen? She skimmed her hand down over her breasts, shivering as she brushed across her sensitive nipples.

Could I even take him? He was just so big—but then again, Alison was even shorter than her and Will was as large as Nakor. Even tiny little Flora had apparently managed a very successful mating with a full-sized orc.

I'd be willing to try, she thought, and smiled as her hand dipped lower and encountered the slickness already coating her folds. Her fingers stroked over her clit, the heat already pulsing through her as she thought of the way his tail had teased her thigh. Would it have climbed higher if he'd let it, maybe even slid inside her wet pussy, preparing her for him?

She slid a finger into the tight entrance, her thumb finding her swollen clit as she imagined him watching her with those glittering amber eyes, demanding that she take him. The image tipped her over, and she cried out as she came, his name echoing through the room before she fell into another deep dreamless sleep.

But despite how well she slept, she woke up with a sense of impending doom.

It was their last day together.

CHAPTER 9

*N*akor woke up frustrated. Frustrated because his cock refused to go down, but also frustrated because he kept dreaming that he was chasing Charlotte through some kind of labyrinth and she was always just out of reach. At first it sounded as if she were laughing at him, but towards morning her muffled noises began to sound more like sobs. That too added to his frustration. He didn't like to think of his little human afraid or unhappy.

Don't be ridiculous, he told himself as he stalked to his shower. He didn't even bother trying to relieve his aching cock—he knew it would stiffen again as soon as she appeared. Still he did his best to pretend that it was simply another workday, dressing in business attire—tailored black pants, a bespoke white shirt, and black suspenders. He chose his favorite Patek Philippe watch, but drew the line at donning a tie.

She will be impressed, he decided, then was immediately annoyed that he was concerned with her opinion.

Unwilling to show his eagerness for her to appear, he set the front door ajar—the first time it had ever been in such a position —and retreated to the kitchen to brew a moody cup of espresso. He knew the moment she entered, but he kept staring out at the sunrise.

"Did I miss a dress code memo?"

Her soft, amused voice did nothing to appease his grumpiness, and he turned and scowled down at her. She was wearing a dress of dark burgundy wool, the rich color a striking contrast to her pale skin. The soft fabric wrapped around her slender curves and showed a teasing hint of skin at the neck. The skirt ended right below her knees, revealing black high-heeled boots. He had a sudden vision of her bent over his desk wearing nothing but those boots, and any hope of controlling his erection disappeared.

"Your clothing is acceptable," he said brusquely, then changed the subject. "Espresso?"

When she nodded, he gratefully turned away to concentrate on measuring the beans and preparing the drink. She watched silently until he handed her the cup and gave her an inquisitive look.

"Do you have any questions this morning?"

"I don't think so."

"Then you can begin. Please," he added. "I have some other matters to take care of."

Without waiting for a response, he stalked through the doors onto the deck and launched himself into the air. He probably looked completely foolish given his present attire, but he needed the clarity of cold air and flight before he did something completely foolish like carry her back to his bedroom, fuck her senseless, and keep her forever.

Fuck.

He did his best to concentrate on flying and taking in deep breaths of the crystalline morning air. When he finally realized he had unconsciously altered his flight path to keep his house in sight at all times, he growled and gave up, swooping back down for a landing.

He found her in his study, and she gave him a quick guilty look when he entered, immediately raising his suspicions.

"What have you been doing?" he growled, and she jumped.

"N-nothing." She twisted her fingers together nervously, then sighed. "I'm afraid I didn't get very much done because I was watching you fly."

Oh. He couldn't help preening. He was an excellent flyer, after all.

"It must be wonderful to be able to do that," she added.

"It is enjoyable. I could take you..."

The words emerged before he could prevent them. *Fuck.* He had absolutely no intention of taking her flying, no matter how delectable it would be to have her pressed against him as he soared towards the clouds... *No.* He opened his mouth to tell her it would never happen, but she looked almost as appalled by the idea as he had been.

"Up in the sky? No, thank you."

The perverse side of his nature immediately wanted to argue.

"Why not? Are you afraid?"

"Yes," she said frankly.

He stalked over to the desk, put his hands on the edge, and leaned towards her.

"You mean you don't trust me?"

A pulse beat wildly in her neck as she licked her lips.

"I didn't say that. Exactly."

"Then what were you saying, sweetheart?" he purred, and her eyes widened behind her glasses before she dropped them to her keyboard.

"Do you want to look at what I've been doing?"

He rubbed the bridge of his nose and accepted the change of subject. It was probably for the best. He grunted and moved over to his side of the desk as she cautiously handed him a folder.

"What is this? I thought you were making notes on the computer."

"It's not the research on the legends, but I thought it might be helpful."

He frowned and opened the folder. It was full of short hand-written notes about his hero and the different aspects of his personality. He'd always thought of Griff as the vehicle for his treasure hunts rather than a character in his own right, but reading through her notes, he realized uncomfortably that more of himself had appeared in his character than he'd intended.

"This is very... interesting, but I'm not sure—"

"Your character is always alone," she interrupted. "Most heroes have friends or sidekicks of some kind. Griff doesn't. He doesn't even have any romantic interests. No one to present his reflection to him. Maybe that's why he can't move forward through the demon realm."

Her cheeks turned pink when he scowled, but she didn't look away.

A sidekick? Griff had never needed any assistance... Except how was he going to get across the Chasm of Doom without an anchor? Unless...

His mind started spinning out possibilities as he sat, only to realize just how close she was. His fingers hesitated over the keyboard. He didn't want anyone, even her, glimpsing his raw words. He shot her a quick look only to find her still watching him, and he cleared his throat.

"Can you work over there by the window?"

"Of course. Or do you want me to leave?"

"No," he said immediately. "Just... move over there."

She nodded, picked up the laptop and more books, and settled herself in the chair by the window. The sunlight struck fiery sparks in her dark hair, distracting him momentarily, but the log jam of words that had built up in his head was breaking free so he pushed aside the pretty sight and bent back over his keyboard.

He worked for the rest of the morning, only stopping when she slid a tray in front of him. A tray with a pile of sandwiches filled with a suspicious-looking substance.

"What is this?"

"Lunch," she said cheerfully.

"I don't recognize this food."

"Your refrigerator left something to be desired. Caviar, gherkins, and champagne do not a meal make."

He crossed his arms and scowled at her.

"It is the finest Osetra caviar."

"I'm sure it is. It's still not lunch. Now eat your tuna salad sandwich."

He gave her an appalled look. "Tuna salad?"

"Yes. And since I used a jar of imported Italian tuna from your pantry to make it, I'm sure it's the very finest tuna. Now eat."

She grinned, grabbed one of the sandwiches, and went back to her chair. The smell was surprisingly enticing. He'd always enjoyed fish, although he usually preferred to swoop down and catch his own. He took a small bite. Despite the unappetizing appearance, the taste was... acceptable.

"Not so bad after all?" She gave him a cheerful grin as she picked up the empty plate. "Now, back to work."

"You do not dictate my work habits."

"Of course not," she said soothingly as she left with the plate.

He frowned after her, tempted to follow her and prove that he was his own dragon, but when he glanced down an awkward phrase struck his eye and he couldn't go any further until it was corrected.

66

The sun was beginning to set when he finally rose and stretched. Charlotte was still curled up in the chair by the window, but her eyes were closed. Her glasses were placed neatly on top of the stack of reference books, and she looked small and vulnerable in her sleep.

For a moment he stood there thinking how right she looked in his chair, in his home, before he shook his head at the fanciful thought.

"Sweetheart... Charlotte."

Her eyes fluttered open, wide and dazed—the same way they had looked after he'd kissed her.

"Oh! Sorry. I must have drifted off."

She tried to sit up and winced.

"Ouch. Cramp."

"Give me your leg," he ordered, dropping down in front of her.

She'd removed her boots, and there was nothing between his fingers and the smooth, silky curve of her calf as he worked the tight muscles.

"Oww, oww, oww... ohh." Her muttered complaints disappeared in a grateful sigh.

"I take it that means I found the right spot?"

"I'll say. I mean, yes." She blushed and quickly changed the subject. "How did it go this afternoon?"

"Very well. I still have some details to work through and a good bit of territory to cover, but I see the way forward."

"That's wonderful. My editor is going to be very happy."

Her smile suddenly wobbled and his fingers tightened at the reminder that she was leaving the next day. *It's for the best.* He would work much faster without a distracting little female around, and yet... He wasn't quite ready to let her go.

"Have dinner with me."

CHAPTER 10

*S*till half-asleep, Charlotte stared up at Nakor, not sure that she'd heard him correctly.

"What?"

"Dinner. The evening meal. Not here with my empty refrigerator," he added with a flash of humor in those amber eyes. "In town."

Part of her was sure it was a bad idea, but for once she ignored that sensible inner voice.

"All right," she whispered.

"Excellent."

He reached for her boots, drawing them up each leg as her heart raced. Who knew that putting on clothing could be almost as erotic as taking it off? His fingers lingered briefly on the sensitive back of her knees, then he rose to his feet, bringing her up with him.

"Do you need to go back to the inn?"

She shook her head.

"Not unless I need to change."

His eyes drifted down over her with an almost palpable heat.

"You are perfect exactly as you are."

Her stomach did a funny little flip, and she bit her lip. *It's just a meal*, she reminded herself as she followed him outside. The sun was setting in a blaze of red and gold glory over the mountains, and she paused for a moment to watch the colors dance across the sky. He came to stand next to her, and she felt the oddest desire to lean back against him and pull his arms around her as they watched.

It's just a meal.

"You like the sunset," he said softly.

She nodded, and his tail crept around her waist, pulling her closer.

"So do I. Even from down here."

They watched until the sun dropped below the horizon, the moment curiously intimate, and she fought back the urge to protest when he finally sighed and his tail dropped away.

When he escorted her across the parking area and opened the passenger door on the Porsche, she almost asked how she would get to work in the morning. Then she remembered that she'd be leaving the next day. It only made sense for him to drop her off at the inn after dinner. Maybe that was why he'd asked her to dinner. Two birds, one stone.

Which is just fine, she told herself fiercely.

"The restaurant is quite small," he warned as he drove swiftly and efficiently down the mountain road.

She managed to force a smile.

"I'm having trouble imagining you cramped up in a normal-sized space."

He gave a half-shrug.

"Perhaps I should have said small in Other terms. And the food is excellent even though the owner is annoying."

Despite the complaint, he sounded amused.

"Annoying?"

"You'll see."

The restaurant was called Midnight Manor, and it was located on a quiet side street a short distance from the town square. It had been converted from a spacious 1920s-era residence, the former parlors now intimate dining areas—intimate for Others. The large minotaur frowning at the empty chair across from him and the equally large orc with the pretty human girlfriend occupied most of one room.

White linen tablecloths adorned the tables, along with a glittering array of crystal and silver. A fire crackled in the fireplace, the hint of smoke mingling with the delicious scent of food. Her stomach growled, and she blushed as the host sauntered towards them.

He had long dark hair, pulled back with a bow, and he was wearing a white linen shirt and black pants tucked into tall black boots. The outfit would have looked theatrical on anyone else, but he wore it so casually that she couldn't imagine him in anything else.

He shot her one swift appraising look, then arched an eyebrow at Nakor.

"Now isn't this a surprise? To what do I owe the honor?"

Nakor shook his head. "We're hungry, of course."

The eyebrow didn't come down. "And you just expect to drop in without a reservation and find a table waiting for you?"

"Damian..."

"Oh, fine. I can probably squeeze you in somewhere." A dazzling smile crossed Damian's face, revealing a pair of extremely sharp fangs. "I have heaters going out on the patio if you think your... companion will be warm enough."

Damian gave her a frankly inquisitive look, but Nakor ignored the implied question as he looked down at her.

"Will that be all right?"

"I'm sure it will be fine. I ate dinner outside with Will and Alison last night."

"Indeed?" Damian led them to the back of the house. "You must be staying at the inn. Their food is quite satisfactory—although not, of course, as good as ours."

The stone-paved patio was nestled between the two wings of the main house, and lush plantings gave it an intimate air. Tiny white bulbs mingled with vines in the overhead trellis, and a fountain bubbled quietly at one end. A werewolf couple lounged by the fountain, but Damian showed them to a table at the other end in front of a glowing chiminea and handed her a soft woolen blanket.

"Since Nakor has apparently forgotten his manners, let me introduce myself. I'm Damian."

"It's nice to meet you. I'm Charlotte."

"How charming." Damian bent down over her hand, pressing cool, soft lips to the back of it, and she shivered. Then he jumped and glared at Nakor. "Stop that. You know how easily I burn."

Smoke was trickling from Nakor's nostrils again. "Then perhaps you shouldn't play with fire."

The two males glared at each other for another moment, then Damian shook his head and grinned.

"I never thought I'd—"

"Be quiet, Damian. Bring us a bottle of champagne and today's menu."

"As you wish." Damian swept an elaborate bow and disappeared.

"He's an... interesting character. Do you know him well?"

"Too well," he said ruefully. "But he has an excellent chef."

"I'm sure he does." She gave him a curious look, wondering if this explained the empty refrigerator. "Do you come here for meals a lot?"

"No. Only occasionally."

"Then what do you usually do for food?"

He looked offended. "I am a dragon. I can hunt."

She tried to imagine someone who had twenty types of tea and his own brand of coffee diving down out of the sky to snap up his dinner and couldn't manage it.

"I'm sure you can," she said politely. "But do you?"

He looked down his nose at her for a moment, then shook his head, lips quirking.

"Of course not. I had a cook for a long time, but she retired to look after her grandchildren."

Does he realize how disgruntled he sounds about that, she wondered, hiding a smile.

"Now I have specially curated meals delivered. They are stored in a refrigerated storage unit in my garage that can be accessed from outside. Which is why I only keep caviar and champagne in the house refrigerator," he added.

"Fine. Next time I'll know to look out there. I mean..."

The subject of her impending departure loomed between them, but before either of them could address it, Damian returned with a bottle of champagne and two crystal glasses.

"I really should have brought three glasses," Damian murmured as he expertly opened the bottle. "But somehow I thought you'd object."

"For once you were right."

Despite the snippy comment, Nakor looked amused again and Damian was clearly unfazed.

"You wound me." He poured the champagne into the glasses with a flourish. "This is from our very own vineyard in northern France. Enjoy."

Nakor snorted as Damian placed two handwritten menus on the table and disappeared, then he lifted his glass in a toast.

"To... unexpected results."

"Hear, hear," she said softly, and took a sip of the champagne. It was exquisite, and she smiled at him across the table.

"This is delicious."

As their eyes met, she found herself trapped in the amber glow of his eyes. The world narrowed down to just the two of them and this single moment of time. A burst of laughter from inside sounded distant and far away, and she found herself leaning towards him, lips parted.

Then he abruptly looked away and the spell was broken. He silently handed her a menu, then studied his own. There were only six options written in an elegant sprawling script—two appetizers, two main courses, and two desserts—but they all sounded delicious.

"One of each?" he suggested. "Or perhaps two?"

Having seen the way he devoured the sandwiches, she nodded.

"That might be better. You need to keep up your strength."

Too late she realized how that sounded. His eyes snapped back to hers as a slow, wicked smile curved his lips.

"That sounds like a challenge."

CHAPTER 11

That shy speculation was remarkably intoxicating, Nakor decided as he watched pink wash over Charlotte's face. Especially when he caught the sweet fragrance of her arousal.

"I mean... I meant for you to have the strength to write," she said, trying to gather her composure.

"Of course you did, sweetheart."

Once again, the endearment slipped out without his consent, but why not? This was his last night with the intriguing little human. The thought annoyed him so he shoved it aside as Damian returned. He ordered, then allowed her to turn the conversation to other subjects.

Perhaps not surprisingly, she was extremely well-read and fascinated with a wide variety of subjects. Their conversation ranged from Byzantine crosses to deforestation in the Amazon as the delicious food was presented to them. He derived almost as much pleasure from watching her eat as he did from his own food, her little sighs of pleasure going directly to his cock.

The main disadvantage of a public venue, even one as discreet as Damian's, was the possibility of being interrupted. The mayor stopped by to discuss improving drainage in the hospital parking lot, but he waved him away impatiently with the promise of a check. He'd noticed the big minotaur was by himself when they arrived and suspected that the other male would have liked to linger, but he had no intention of including a third person in their evening.

"Who was that?" Charlotte asked, her eyes wide as she watched the mayor leave.

Was that admiration on her face? He frowned.

"Just the mayor. We call him Houston," he added reluctantly, realizing belatedly that he probably should have introduced her.

"Houston?"

"He's the first one anyone calls when they have a problem."

She stared at him for a moment before she started laughing.

"Poor man, I mean, male."

"He chose the job." He shrugged and directed the conversation back to more interesting matters.

They lingered over their coffees—not as good as his of course—long after the werewolf couple had departed, leaving them alone on the patio. The fire in the chiminea had faded to embers when he saw her shiver.

"You're cold."

"Maybe a little."

"Why didn't you say something?" Foolish little human. "Come here."

She looked at his outstretched hand for a long moment. He opened his mouth to demand that she obey, but he suddenly found himself wanting her to make the choice. After another second's hesitation, she placed her hand in his. Warmth rippled through his chest as he gently tugged her up from her seat and down onto his lap.

She perched there hesitantly, placing her hand cautiously against his chest for balance, then sighed with pleasure.

"You're so warm."

Her hand was freezing against his skin and something that felt uncomfortably like guilt washed over him. He should have been paying closer attention. He made an impatient sound and pulled her firmly back against his chest, wrapping both arms around her and resting his chin on top of her head.

"Is that better?"

"So much better." She tucked her cold nose into his neck, still shivering as the heat of his body penetrated.

"You should have told me you were cold."

She leaned back to give him an indignant look.

"Wait a minute. You're annoyed because *I'm* cold?"

"Yes. It was foolish of you not to let me know the temperature wasn't suitable. Humans are very fragile." Not that she felt fragile at the moment. She felt cool and soft and extraordinarily tempting as her attempts to snuggle closer made her ass rub repeatedly against his cock. "Now be still."

She obeyed with a disgruntled huff as he brought his wings around her as well.

Fuck. Why did she have to feel so perfect in his arms? She was leaving tomorrow. The unexpected ache in his chest annoyed him even more.

"I should take you back to the inn so you can warm up," he said reluctantly.

"I'm not cold at all now."

Her hand slid up, stroking his throat, and desire slammed into him with enough force to take his breath away. He knew he should ignore the temptation, but he couldn't resist. He drew his hand down over her body, skimming lightly over the soft knit covering her slender curves as he tugged her tighter against his aching cock.

A soft gasp escaped her pretty lips, but she didn't make any attempt to stop him as he cupped her breast. Instead, she arched against his hand and he drew a claw lightly across the stiff point of her nipple. She shuddered, and he couldn't resist sliding his hand down to her knee and then up under the skirt. As he trailed his hand along her thigh, her legs parted to allow him access, and he purred with satisfaction.

"Do you want me, sweetheart?" he growled. "Say you want me."

"I... I..." She looked up at him, the grey eyes behind her glasses silver in the moonlight, then nodded. "Yes. I want you."

Triumph roared through him as he lowered his head and kissed her. She sighed against his mouth, then responded to him with the same passionate intensity as their previous kiss. His wings flexed, preparing to take flight, to carry her back to his cave —*house*—but she was human and she was afraid of flying.

Human. The thought made him break the kiss momentarily, but looking down at her flushed face and swollen lips erased his doubts. He wanted her—and she wanted him too.

"More," she whispered. "Please."

That last word did it.

"I intend to give you everything you want, sweetheart."

The words rang a little too true, but he ignored that uncomfortable fact as he rose with her still in his arms and carried her through the deserted restaurant. He caught a brief glimpse of Damian out of the corner of his eye, but apparently the vampire valued his life enough not to intercede.

The car was too small to allow him to keep her on his lap—a regrettable lack of foresight on his part—but he kept her tucked against his side as he drove home at a speed that would have been reckless for any other driver. She didn't object, just closed her eyes and burrowed against him, her hand tracing tantalizing patterns over his chest. The one time she dipped lower, he wrenched the steering wheel so hard that they almost left the road. She confined her touch to the area above his waist after that.

As soon as they arrived at his home, he swept her inside and headed straight to his bedroom. He could have taken her anywhere—a couch, a table, hell, even the wall would have worked—but this was her first time with him. He wanted to do it properly.

She stiffened in his arms as she saw the bed and he slowed, just in case she was having second thoughts. *Please don't let her be having second thoughts.*

"Is something wrong?"

"Umm, no. It's just a very large bed."

"I am a very large male. The mattress is custom made from hand-clipped Argentinian horse hair."

"Of course it is."

She rolled her eyes, her face softening. He waited for another moment, but she remained relaxed in his arms and he carried her over to the bed and put her down.

"Now what?"

She gave him a smile that was half-shy, half-demanding, and he purred as he went down on his knees in front of her. He parted her legs, the dress falling to the sides to reveal a tiny scrap of red silk.

"Now we get rid of this."

She gulped as he ripped it away with a quick twist of his claws.

"Those were... Oh!"

She gasped as he yanked her closer, covering the entire length of her tempting little slit with his tongue. Sweetness flooded his tongue as he groaned and began to explore, moving from the swollen pearl of her clit to the tiny entrance to her body, licking and teasing until she was trembling, on the verge of climax, and then he stood up and stripped off his clothing.

CHAPTER 12

*C*harlotte's heart beat a tattoo of anticipation as Nakor ripped off his clothes, anticipation mixed with perhaps the tiniest hint of trepidation despite the arousal humming through her veins. The fine gold scales on his heavily muscled torso gleamed as his shirt fluttered to the ground, making him look even larger and more intimidating than usual. Keeping those glittering amber eyes on her face, he stripped away his pants.

Oh my God.

The thick cock emerging from the slit at the base of his abdomen was as golden as the rest of his skin and huge, with a thick ridge that spiraled the entire length from base to tip. As she stared, open-mouthed, an opalescent drop pearled on the tip. It was impossible not to reach out and brush her fingertip over the tempting drop. Nakor groaned and she immediately snatched her hand away.

"Don't stop," he ordered, moving closer as she lifted her finger to her mouth.

Mmm. Sweet and spicy, like cinnamon honey.

She grasped his cock, a molten bar in her hands, and sought out another drop directly from the tip. More of the sweet spiciness flooded her mouth, and she realized his entire shaft was slick, her finger moving easily as she followed that spiraling ridge. He groaned again, his hips jerking towards her, then stepped back. He lifted her to her feet long enough to strip off her clothes, then flung her back on to the bed and came down over her.

His wings flared, blocking out everything else as the heat of his body surrounded her, and the subtle texture of his scales grazed teasingly across her aching breasts. He gently removed her glasses, then paused, looking down at her. Amber eyes glowed as he studied her, the mixture of emotions on his face impossible for her to read.

"Do you want this?" he asked, a note of uncertainty beneath his usual arrogance.

"Yes."

There was no doubt in her mind. He might be arrogant and bossy and... well, a dragon, but there was no one else she had ever wanted like this. She knew there was no future for the two of them, and she suspected this was only going to make it harder to walk away from him, but she also knew she would never forgive herself if she didn't take this chance.

She raised her hand and stroked the sharp edges of his cheekbones, and the next moment he was kissing her, his tongue driving into her mouth as his hands stroked over her breasts, tweaking her sensitive nipples, and down over her belly to her slick pussy.

A low rumbling growl vibrated through his chest as he stroked a finger up and down over her folds, circling her entrance without going inside. She arched up, desperate for more, and he obliged, that broad fingertip sliding just inside before withdrawing again.

"Hurry."

"You are very small."

There was that note of doubt again, but he pushed his finger deeper and she moaned, raising herself against his hand.

"Not too small."

He growled, rising above her on his knees, her legs spread wide around his powerful thighs. She'd almost forgotten just how massive he was, but before she had a chance to worry about whether or not she could actually take him, he slowly pushed forward and in.

Pressure. Fullness. Burning that tipped the edge into pain... And then he was in, his thick cock buried to the hilt inside her. Her muscles contracted, clamping around the massive invader, and they both moaned.

"Fuck."

The harsh curse coming from those haughty lips almost made her giggle, but before the sound could escape, he withdrew, that thick ridge scraping the sensitive inside of her channel and making her see stars. Her laugh turned into a cry as he pushed back in, her body adjusting to him as he stroked out and in again, each movement going a little deeper than before, opening her a little more.

It felt so good she couldn't breathe, her hands clinging to him, fingernails digging into his shoulders as he moved over her, the powerful muscles in his arms flexing with each thrust. His wings blocked out everything except the fire burning in those amber eyes as his cock stretched her open, helpless beneath him like some ancient sacrifice. His hips thrust faster and faster until her pleasure exploded and her inner muscles gripped him in long, pulsing waves as she came and came and came.

He kept moving as her climax rolled on, building a blazing inferno of desire that grew and grew until she suddenly peaked again and he shouted her name, driving deep, the thick band around his shaft swelling as he came.

For a long, endless moment, he remained locked inside her. She couldn't move, could barely think, but it didn't matter. He was there, surrounding her, possessing her, and it was good.

So incredibly, blissfully good.

She had never even imagined any physical encounter could be quite so overwhelming.

A soft sigh escaped her lips, and he gathered her against his chest, curling on his side with his arms around her, his tail curved over her leg, and his cock still embedded deep within her. She snuggled closer, running her fingers across the subtle pattern of his scales.

"I'm not sure I'm going to be able to move tomorrow."

"Then don't."

Her heart skipped a beat at the tempting thought, but she shook her head.

"My flight is tomorrow. I might have to settle for a heating pad. Of course, you're kind of like one big heating pad."

She did her best to make her laugh sound natural, and he nipped lightly at the curve of her shoulder.

"Do I amuse you?" he demanded, sounding more grumpy than angry.

"Maybe a little bit."

A startled laugh rumbled through his chest, vibrating her own body as he finally withdrew, taking care not to hurt her.

"You will stay with me tonight."

It was a command, not a request, but since she had no desire to leave, she let it go.

She expected to fall asleep quickly, but although her body was limp and sated, her mind refused to turn off. She looked out at the dimly lit room, furnished like the rest of the house in sleek, expensive elegance.

"Did you build this house?"

"Yes. It is a... tradition that each dragon builds his own cave —*house*—when he reaches adulthood."

"Do your parents live near here?"

She half-expected him not to answer the question, but he answered easily enough.

"No. My mother is in Greece, and my father is in Transylvania."

"Transylvania? Really? Like in all those Dracula movies?"

Or was that a stereotype?

"Yes. He's there with Damian's father. They're partners. That's why I know Damian so well. He's like an annoying half-brother."

"Oh." Now that he said it, she understood why their banter seemed so familiar. "And your mother?"

"Was a very well compensated female. My grandfather insisted that the family line should continue and she made it possible. Now she has a very nice villa on the side of an extinct volcano and a bevy of young male attendants."

He sounded amused rather than annoyed, and she gave him a curious look.

"It doesn't bother you?"

"No. She was a good mother when I was young. I suppose she's still a good mother, although we don't see each other that often. Then again, most dragons prefer to live alone."

"Even if they're... mated?"

"A mated dragon is even less likely to appear in public—he's too busy with his mate."

His eyes started to heat again, but she wasn't through with her questions.

"Do you see your father?"

"Also not often, although unlike my mother, he and his partner come back here occasionally. There aren't any bad feelings between us, we just lead different lives."

"I know what that's like," she said quietly. "My mom died when I was young, and for a long time it was just me and my dad. Then when I was in high school he got married again and started a new family. I think he'd started to realize he would be on his own once I went off to college."

"Do you not get along with your stepmother?"

"She's fine, and their kids are cute, but... it never felt like my family. We exchange cards and calls on the holidays, but that's about it."

"You have a dragon family too," he said softly.

She knew he was talking about the distance between her and the rest of her family, but she couldn't help wishing for something more—an actual family with her dragon.

Just one night, she reminded herself, and reached between their bodies to tease his cock, determined to take advantage of every moment.

CHAPTER 13

*N*akor had heard the expression "the scales fell from his eyes" before, but he had never truly appreciated it until tonight. The slender human now sleeping in his arms after he drew another long string of climaxes from her was a revelation in every possible way.

Just the memory of her delicate pink flesh opening for him as he drove into her small body had his cock stiffening once again. He licked his lips, savoring her taste, already hungry for more. The sound of her voice crying out his name was the finest music he'd ever heard, but the soft sighs she made in her sleep as she snuggled trustingly in his arms helped soothe his raging lust.

Lust? No, it was more than that. Her perceptive mind, her warmth, even her streak of stubborn human determination—all of them added to her appeal, like the facets on a perfectly cut stone. He wanted to keep her, to add her to his hoard like the rare and valuable jewel she was.

I can't keep her.

The thought made him frown, but unfortunately the days when a dragon could carry a maiden off to his cave and lock her away were long gone. But perhaps there were more... modern equivalents.

As soon as the first faint light of dawn touched the horizon, he slipped out of bed, tucking her down amongst the pillows before striding away to his study. When he returned half an hour later, the sun had started to rise, the warm morning light casting a rosy glow over her normally pale skin.

He bent over and kissed her like the sleeping princess she resembled. Her lips parted beneath his before her eyes fluttered open, heavy-lidded with sleep and pleasure.

"Good morning," she whispered. "Is it time to get up?"

He smiled, his lips brushing against hers again. "Not quite."

Before she could ask, he lifted her into his arms. She squeaked and clung to his neck as he carried her through into the bathroom, using his tail to keep her securely on his hip while he turned on the shower and checked the temperature, adjusting it for her delicate human skin. He would have to program a setting for her. Or simply insist that she take every shower with him. *An acceptable alternative*, he decided as he carried her under the jets.

He purred with delight as her arms tightened around his neck before she threw her head back under one of the sprays, laughing with delight. An excellent idea. He lifted her higher, high enough to lick drops of water from her pert little nipple. She squirmed and winced and arched against his mouth all at the same time.

"Nakor... I don't think... Mmm."

The first moan ended in a gasp as he spun her around.

"Put your arms up around my neck," he ordered, adjusting his grip to hold her thighs apart as he angled her body towards one of the jets.

She writhed against him as the pulsating stream danced across her swollen pink pearl, sending her flying with shocking speed as his cock throbbed helplessly against her ass. When she waved a limp hand at him, he took pity and moved her away from the spray.

"Wow. No wonder you were so pissed when I interrupted your shower," she murmured as she sagged against him. Then her eyes widened. "Wait a minute. Were you...?"

"Trying to relieve my aching cock? Yes. I'd spent the night dreaming about a very annoying and very beautiful human female."

She blushed, her eyes dropping to his erection.

"It looks like you need more relief."

"I don't think you're quite ready for more, sweetheart," he said regretfully.

"I don't mind waiting while you, err, take care of things."

A small pink tongue flicked across her lips, and that was almost enough to push him over.

"Indeed. Perhaps you could even be of assistance."

He placed her soft little fingers on his cock, then covered them with his hand, showing her how to use the twisting motion that followed the spiraled ridge. She mimicked him eagerly, stepping closer so that the head of his cock brushed tormentingly against her soft stomach each time it flexed. Her tongue peeked out again as she concentrated on the move, an adorably intent expression on her small face.

The world narrowed to that one point of contact as her hand moved faster, his climax racing towards him with embarrassing speed.

"Look at me," he demanded, and her eyes snapped up to his as he roared, climaxing in long, powerful spurts against her stomach, his seed glistening gold on her pale skin.

She whimpered, and he slid his hand down over her still tender folds, knowing he'd find her hot and wet. Her fingers tightened around him, milking another pulse from his cock as he rubbed the heel of his hand against her swollen clit. She cried out as she came once more, her whole body shuddering. He held her close until she stopped quivering, then switched off the shower and toweled them both dry with his imported Egyptian cotton bath sheets.

"Time to go back to bed."

She didn't try and object until he put her back down on the mattress, then she quickly stood back up, shaking her head.

"I wish I could, but I can't. I have to go back to the inn and pack and get ready for my flight. I'll have to arrange for a car to the airport as well."

"You don't need to worry about any of those things," he said smugly, and she gave him a puzzled frown.

"What do you mean? Were you planning to take me to the airport? That would be awfully nice if you could spare the time, but I hate to take you away from your writing now that it's flowing again."

"You won't be taking me away from my writing because I won't be going anywhere. Neither will you."

She actually sighed and patted his arm, repeating her words as if he were incapable of understanding.

"I'm glad that you don't want me to leave but I have to go. My flight is today."

"Your flight was today," he corrected. "It has been changed to two weeks from today."

He had started to demand longer, but some remnant of his usual caution had agreed that a trial period might be preferable. Even if she did leave at the end of this period, he had no intention of subjecting her to the vagaries of commercial flight, but he'd decided that that battle could wait as well.

"You changed my flight?"

"No, your editor—Marjorie?—changed it. I called her this morning and explained that I needed you here in order to continue making progress on my book. She agreed. You're now working for me."

CHAPTER 14

"*I*'m what?"

Charlotte stared up at the huge, betraying bastard, unable to believe her ears. Or, more accurately, all too afraid to believe her ears.

"Working for me," he said patiently. "We decided that it would make more sense to have you reporting to me while you're down here. In fact, I think you should just go ahead and move in with me so that you're always available."

"Available? You unmitigated bastard."

Her ears were ringing she was so furious, and she hauled off and slapped him across his big, smug, annoyingly handsome face. He actually had the nerve to look shocked, covering the place where she'd slapped him as if there had been any chance that she'd hurt him.

"Why are you so angry?"

"Hmm, well, let me see. You made a decision about me, a decision that affects my job, without consulting me. You seem to think that you're now my so-called boss—" and yes, she used air quotes "—and I'm therefore available to you whenever you want. I'm not your fucking whore."

He looked so genuinely appalled that she almost softened, but then his face hardened into the familiar arrogant lines.

"I thought nothing of the kind. I have never paid for a female, and I certainly do not intend to start now, especially with—"

He broke off, glaring at her.

"With a human? Is that what you were going to say?" she asked, her voice dripping with artificial sweetness.

"No," he snarled, but he didn't complete his original sentence.

"I don't believe you."

The smoke started trickling from his nose again, but she ignored it, searching desperately for her clothes. She had the horrible feeling that once her anger faded it would be replaced by tears. She threw her dress over her head without bothering to search for the remnants of her underwear, jammed her glasses on her nose, picked up her boots, and stalked towards the door.

"Where are you going?"

"Away from here."

"In my car?" he asked, his voice low and dangerous.

"I have no intention of touching your fucking car. I'll walk down the damn mountain."

She made it as far as the porch, struggling to stand upright while she tried to pull on her boots, before he caught up with her. He'd yanked on a pair of jeans, and she did her best not to notice how closely they molded to those muscular thighs.

"You are not walking down the damn mountain."

"Why not?"

"Because your delicate little human ass will probably end up falling off a cliff or getting eaten by bears or lost."

None of those possible fates had crossed her mind—until now—but she gave him a defiant look anyway.

"I'll be just fine."

"Get in the damn car."

She put her hands on her hips and glared at him. "And if I don't?"

Was that actually a puff of flame shooting out of his nostril this time? Maybe challenging an angry dragon wasn't the best idea.

"If you don't..." He leaned down so his face was only inches away from hers—and why did she suddenly want to kiss that forbidding scowl? "If you don't, I will pick you up and fly you back to town myself."

"You wouldn't dare."

His wings flared. "Try me."

She glared at him for another minute, then turned and stalked off towards the car. As she did, she realized that her nipples were stiff, aching points and her clit was throbbing in a slow, steady pulse of arousal. How could she be so angry and so turned on at the same time?

She climbed into the car and crossed her arms over her chest, trying to surreptitiously ease the ache as he joined her. He slammed the door, but as he pressed the start button, his head suddenly swiveled towards her. Amber eyes glowed.

"You're aroused."

"I am nothing of the kind."

His lips curved into a much too arrogant smile as she seethed silently, but to her surprise he didn't say anything. They made the journey in complete silence, although she was well aware that he was driving more slowly than he had previously. He turned through the gates of the inn, but instead of driving up to the building, he pulled to one side, sighed, and turned to face her.

"It is possible that I did not think this through," he said stiffly.

"You think?" she muttered, but he kept going.

"I did not—do not—equate the two... aspects of our relationship. You have been helpful with my book, surprisingly helpful, and I would like for you to continue assisting me." He hesitated, and his tail crept tentatively around her ankle. "The... attraction between us has nothing to do with your job. I simply thought that your being here would allow us to spend more time together."

It made a twisted kind of sense, but...

"It never occurred to you to discuss it with me, did it? Either part?"

"I assumed you—"

His mouth slammed shut, and he threw the door open, tossing the keys to her as he climbed out.

"This is pointless. If you wish to work, you know where to find me."

He launched himself into the air before she could respond, his golden figure disappearing into the sky.

He didn't even mention the personal side of their relationship—if you could call it a relationship.

Ignoring the ache in her chest, she moved around to the driver's side and drove the rest of the way up to the inn. Somehow she wasn't surprised to find Flora waiting on the porch when she trudged up the steps.

"Male trouble, dear?"

"Nothing but."

"Hmm." Flora studied her through those far too discerning dark eyes, but to Charlotte's surprise, she didn't ask any questions. "You know what you need?"

"No. What?" She couldn't quite keep the trepidation out of her tone.

"A girls' night. Why wait until tomorrow night?"

"I'm not really in the mood. And I've never been the party ty—"

"Nonsense." Flora completely ignored her protest. "This is just what you need. I'll make all the arrangements. See you later, dear."

Flora whisked herself away, leaving Charlotte staring after her with her mouth open. Damn. The last thing she wanted to do was put on a cheerful act for anyone. She'd just have to find Flora later and tell her firmly that she wasn't going anywhere.

She suspected it would be easier said than done, but the combination of very little sleep and an emotional morning was crashing down on her and she was too exhausted to worry about it. She dragged herself upstairs to her room, took a very hot—and very lonely—shower, pretending that the water on her face was only from the faucet, and climbed wearily into bed.

After a brief debate with herself, she decided not to call Marjorie. Not only was she convinced that her editor would insist she go along with whatever Nakor wanted, whining about the decision wouldn't help her already teetering career. She expected those rapidly diminishing job prospects to keep her awake. Instead, she fell asleep so quickly it was almost like falling under a spell.

By the time she woke, the afternoon shadows were already beginning to slant through the trees lining the drive, but she felt a hundred times better. Not that anything had changed—it just no longer seemed so dark and depressing.

"I suppose I might as well see what Flora is up to," she muttered, then pulled on jeans and a cozy sweater and headed downstairs.

When she peeped cautiously around the door to the sunroom behind the kitchen, she found Alison alone.

"Is Flora around?" she whispered.

The other woman laughed.

"I haven't seen her, but that doesn't mean anything. She can appear and disappear almost like—"

"Magic," she finished and Alison laughed again.

"Exactly. Why are you looking for her?"

"She said something about a girls' night out." She twisted her fingers together. "I'd love to some other time, but I really don't want to go anywhere tonight."

"So that's what she's up to."

Alison frowned thoughtfully, and Charlotte's heart sank.

"What?"

"Oh, nothing bad. At least I don't think so. If you'd rather just stay here, that's absolutely fine, but Elara invited us over to her coffee shop to try out some new coffee and cupcake flavors."

"Elara?"

"She's human too—mated to Flora's grandson, Grondar."

"And it's just coffee and cupcakes?" That definitely sounded more her speed right now than a drunken night out, no matter how pleasant the company.

"That's all. And Grondar is the absolute best baker in town. But no pressure."

Her stomach growled as Alison gave her a hopeful smile.

"I suppose. I mean, that's very nice of you to invite me," she added quickly.

"Excellent. Just let me tell Ginger I'm leaving."

"Ginger?"

"Our latest guest."

"I don't think I've seen her."

"That doesn't surprise me. I think she's only left her room twice since she arrived." Alison frowned. "I'll ask her too, but I don't think she'll come."

Sure enough, she returned alone, still frowning.

"I wish I knew if she needed help, but Flora just told me to leave her alone."

"She probably already knows her entire life story," she muttered as she pulled on a scarf.

"Probably." Alison tugged a woolen hat down over her curls and smiled at her. "But she never means any harm."

"That would be more reassuring if I were convinced our definition of harm is the same."

Alison's smile turned rueful as they set out.

"Unfortunately, I suspect you're right."

As they walked through the gathering dusk, Charlotte asked, "You mentioned that Elara is mated to one of Flora's grandsons. Does she have more than one?"

"Yes and no. Grondar is her own daughter's son, while Trogar and Holder are her sister's grandsons, but they all call her Gran. It's funny—all three of them could break her with a single pinky, and all three of them are terrified of her. They adore her as well," she added hastily. "But what she says goes."

"Nakor seems to feel the same way."

The words popped out without thinking, and Alison shot her a sideways glance at the bitterness in her voice.

"Do you want to talk about it?"

"No. Yes. I don't know. We had a disagreement this morning." She sighed. "More than a disagreement. He just arbitrarily decided I should move in with him and work for him too, and went behind my back to my boss."

Alison gave a low whistle.

"I've dated a few of those uber control freaks in my time. It never ends well. That is..."

"What?"

"It never ends well with humans. The Others are... different. Will is super bossy, but in the best possible way." Her voice turned dreamy. "They all seem to have this urge to protect their mates."

"Mate?" she squeaked. "No one said anything about mates."

For a second Alison's eyes were almost as penetrating as Flora's, but then she smiled and shook her head.

"I'm probably just projecting my own experiences. Now hurry up or all the cupcakes will be gone."

"Gone? Why would they be—"

Her question died away as they emerged onto Main Street, the brick storefronts glowing in the light of the flickering gas lanterns. The coffee shop was directly across the street, and she could already see several women moving around inside.

"It really is a cupcake tasting," Alison said quickly. "And it's not a bar. But there may be a few cocktails."

Charlotte sighed and followed her across the street.

CHAPTER 15

*A*ggravating, infuriating, annoying, delicious female.

Nakor growled, pacing back and forth across his living room. He'd been working all day—or rather trying to work. The words that had flowed so easily yesterday had disappeared with Charlotte.

Normally the sunset would have called to him, but tonight he didn't even spare it a glance. Part of him just wanted to forget the whole disturbing incident, but a much larger part wanted to swoop back down to the inn and bring her back here where she belonged. Did she not realize that no other person had ever set foot inside his cave—*house*—before?

And to have that honor thrown back in his face... To have made the foolish mistake of thinking that his feelings were reciprocated... He wished the ache in his chest was just from his damaged pride.

"Pride goeth before a fall," Flora said piously.

He swore under his breath and turned to find her perched outside on one of his deck chairs. Not that he had any idea how she'd managed to make her way onto the deck without him seeing her.

"This is private property," he snapped, and her eyes narrowed.

"Don't you get snippy with me, boy. I used to change your diapers."

It might have been true; it might not. Baby dragons had a disconcerting tendency to spit up fire at anyone they weren't related to—but he doubted that would have stopped Flora.

"Of course, I had the sense to change out those ridiculous Belgian linen ones for the store-bought kind."

He winced. That definitely had the ring of truth.

"That was a long time ago."

"Doesn't mean you don't still need someone watching your ass." She cackled at her own joke while he waited as patiently as possible for her merriment to subside.

"What do you want, Flora?"

"To tell you not to fuck this up. I should have realized you'd act like a typical blind male dragon. Charlotte's a sweet girl. A smart girl. Better than you deserve."

"I am an Earlsworth."

"A lonely Earlsworth," she snapped back, then shrugged. "But maybe she'll find a better prospect."

"What do you mean—a better prospect?"

Her grin was pure malicious enjoyment.

"I sent her out with Alison and Elara and Nichola."

"You didn't."

"I most certainly did. Four pretty young females—sure to attract a lot of attention. So put that in your pipe and smoke it." She cackled again, then abruptly sobered. "She's the right one, Nakor, but you will have to prove yourself worthy."

She disappeared around the corner of the house before he could come back with a retort, and he growled.

How dare she send Charlotte out with anyone? She was his. The sooner she figured that out, the better.

He took a step towards the edge of the balcony, his wings unfurling, then froze. If he went after her now, she would just accuse him of trying to control her again. Of acting like an over-bearing, overprotective idiot. And it was just possible she could be right.

Fuck.

He needed help. Someone he could trust. He trusted Damian, especially given their familial ties, but he didn't think the vampire had ever taken a female seriously. Which left him with exactly one other option. He sighed and took to the air, studiously avoiding the urge to go in search of his annoyingly little female. What if she needed him? What if she were in danger?

Don't be ridiculous. Not only was Fairhaven Falls a remarkably safe place, Flora—whatever her faults—would never allow any harm to come to Charlotte. Instead, he landed in Trogar's yard again.

"Twice in two days. This is becoming a habit."

The orc's voice did not suggest that it was a favorable one, but Nakor ignored his friend's habitual grumpiness.

"I need... help."

The word wanted to stick in his throat, and Trogar gave him a thoughtful look before relenting enough to toss him a beer.

"It's obviously not about money, so what kind of help?"

"I need help with a... female. A human female. She thinks that I'm an arrogant, controlling asshole and she won't listen to me."

The orc laughed, an unexpectedly deep, humorous sound in the darkness.

"In other words, she sees your true nature? I don't see the problem."

He took two strides across the yard, then back again.

"I think she may be the one."

He carefully avoided looking at his friend.

Silence greeted him, then Trogar asked cautiously, "Do you mean your mate?"

"Yes."

"Uh, congratulations."

"I would appreciate more enthusiasm."

Trogar shrugged. "It's not a fate I ever wished for myself. Human, you say?"

He growled, and Trogar's laughter rolled out again.

"I have nothing against them other than the fact that they're so ridiculously small. But Grondar seems happy enough with his." The orc rubbed his chin thoughtfully. "So no mating flight."

"No." He ignored a tiny flicker of sadness at the thought. Every dragon was brought up to believe that their mating flight would be the highlight of their life. But the reality of having Charlotte in his arms was far better than a theoretical mating flight.

"I assume you're not interested in a mating run, like the wolves do? I've heard it's a lot of fun."

"A mating run? That sounds barbaric. Mating is private and sacred."

"That's not the point."

He sighed and joined Trogar on the porch, grabbing another beer.

"What is the point?"

"It is a way to indicate your claim. Have you told her that she is your mate?"

"I'm sure it's obvious."

"To a human?" Trogar asked skeptically.

Wasn't it obvious? He had brought her into his territory. Into his cave—*house*. He had fed her the finest food and champagne. *And she gave me tuna salad.*

"Perhaps not," he admitted.

"In that case, the first thing you need to do is show her how you feel."

"How I feel? She is quite aware of her effect on me."

He couldn't help sounding a little smug as he remembered the previous night, but Trogar sighed.

"I'm not talking about your goddamn dick. I mean courting her."

"Courting her? How?"

"I'm not entirely sure," Trogar admitted, and he threw his beer can at him.

"Thanks. That's a big help."

"I told you it wasn't my area. How did your parents get together?"

"My father gave my mother an unnumbered Swiss bank account and a set of Empress Josephine's diamonds."

"Would that work on your female?"

"Since she already accused me of trying to buy her, I doubt it," he said dryly.

They sat in silence for several minutes as he gloomily tried to understand what would appeal to a female who rejected large sums of money.

"What about presents?" Trogar asked finally. "Gran always liked presents."

"Isn't that just another form of transaction?"

"What was it she used to say? That the thought was more important than the cost?"

What an appalling idea. But perhaps it would appeal to her warped human sensibilities.

"Very well. I will try to discover such an oddity." He rose to his feet, then nodded abruptly at his friend. "Thank you, Trogar."

"That's all right." The orc shuddered. "Better you than me. But if you figure out how to win her over, I reckon you can bring her by."

Since Trogar valued his privacy as much as Nakor, it was a surprising offer, and he thanked his friend gravely before taking flight.

As he winged his way back to his home—with no more than the briefest circle over town—he did his best to think of something with low dollar value and great sentimental value. An impossible task, but he was determined to succeed. Charlotte would be his.

Now he simply needed to figure out how to convince her.

CHAPTER 16

"You humans are such lightweights," Nichola complained as she steered Charlotte back on to the sidewalk.

Nichola was Will's sister—a tall blue-skinned troll with fluffy orange hair, a friendly smile, and a wicked sense of humor. She'd been playing bartender all night.

The evening had turned out much better than she'd anticipated. All of the women, human and Other, had been friendly and welcoming, extolling the virtues of Fairhaven Falls. No one seemed to pay any attention to her protests that she was just there for a few weeks, and she eventually stopped trying. She just enjoyed the camaraderie, the truly excellent food, and the outrageous stories.

At least she thought they were stories. A yeti wouldn't really have snowboarded down Main Street. Would he?

"I warned you about Nichola's drinks," Alison said, her walk only a little straighter than Charlotte's.

"I know you did. I didn't have any cocktails."

"None of them?"

"No. I figured tomorrow—well, today now—was going to be hard enough. I just had a few of those extra yummy milkshakes," she added as she took a wide path around the bush that tried to leap out and attack her.

"Oh, those," Nichola said innocently, and Alison sighed.

"What did you put in them?"

"Nothing much. Cream. Chocolate syrup. Maybe a tiny smidge of vodka. A little bit of coffee liqueur. Some coconut rum. Oh, and a little kirsch, just for flavor."

"In other words, what didn't you put in them?" Alison grabbed Charlotte's arm. "I'm sorry, Charlotte. She just can't help herself."

"I can, but I wanted Charlotte to have some fun and not spend the evening worrying about Mr. Big Dick Dragon."

"He does have a big dick," she sighed, and the other two started laughing.

"I meant he was a big jerk, but I'll take that interpretation." Nichola waggled her fluffy orange eyebrows. "Care to tell us more?"

"I don't need to hear the details."

Alison rolled her eyes and urged Charlotte to start walking again. She had come to a halt, thinking wistfully about Nakor and his undeniable skills.

"He's a double big dick," she decided.

"You know, the nagas actually have two dicks," Nichola said thoughtfully. "It can be very entertaining."

Alison groaned and put her hand over her face.

"Do you know how Will would react if he ever heard you say that?"

Nichola laughed and shook her finger at Alison. "As amusing as it would be to find out, remember that what happens on girl's night, stays on girl's night."

"Trust me, I wasn't planning on telling him. He still has illusions about you."

Charlotte sighed as the other two continued teasing each other. Despite the pretty little glow currently hovering around her, she was still going to have to decide what to do tomorrow morning—no, *this* morning. Should she go ahead and work with the betraying bastard? Run back to New York with her tail between her legs and probably lose her job? Or maybe just hide away in her room for the next two weeks like the mysterious Ginger?

The last option seemed like the most preferable, especially after Alison and Nichola escorted her back to the inn and made sure she was safely tucked into bed before heading to Alison's cottage, accompanied by Nichola's enthusiastic rendering of "Girls Just Want to Have Fun."

As she drifted off to sleep, she could swear she heard the words echoing down the mountain.

The next morning was considerably less pleasant.

"I knew that third milkshake was a bad idea," she moaned to her reflection in the bathroom mirror as her stomach danced an unhappy little jig.

She downed three painkillers and a glass of water before staggering back to bed. She didn't even have a chance to pull the covers over her head before there was a knock on the door, immediately followed by a beaming Flora carrying a tray. *Didn't I lock that door?*

"Good morning, dear," Flora said cheerfully as she whisked through the door. This morning she was wearing a vivid fuchsia tracksuit that was far too bright for Charlotte's current state. "I heard you were feeling a little under the weather."

"Thanks to you and your cupcake tasting," she muttered, sitting back up with a resigned sigh.

"You were in good hands with Nichola," the older woman said serenely as she put the tray on the table by the window and picked up a glass of disgusting-looking green liquid. "This will help."

"What is it?"

"Just a little something my friend Gladys brewed up. Swallow it all down in one big gulp."

The thought made her stomach churn again, but Flora's gaze was remarkably compelling and she reluctantly obeyed. Once her head returned to its proper place on her shoulders, she realized that her stomach had settled and the drink had left a pleasant, lingering warmth.

"Your friend Gladys is a genius."

Flora gave her a complacent smile.

"I know. She's taken top witch in the Southeast three years running. Jeremiah is her only real competition, and of course, he won't compete against her anymore."

Witch?

She was still turning that over as Flora propped up the pillows behind her, then placed the tray on her lap.

"Scrambled eggs, toast, and fruit. Now eat up. You'll need your strength."

The memory of saying that to Nakor immediately flashed through her mind, and she started to push the tray away.

"Now, now. None of that," Flora said firmly. "If women stopped eating every time a male behaved stupidly, we'd all fade away from starvation."

That surprised a choked laugh from her, and she picked up a piece of toast, hot, buttery, and delicious. Her appetite came roaring back and she ate hungrily as Flora poured her a cup of tea—plain, strong English breakfast tea—then sipped thoughtfully at her own cup while Charlotte ate.

"Now, dear. What are you going to do?"

She sighed.

"I suppose I'm going to go back to the house to be his assistant —*just* his assistant. I really would like to help him finish the book."

"Excellent. I think that's a very wise decision. However..."

The wicked twinkle in Flora's eyes alarmed her.

"However what?"

"I think Nakor needs to realize that his wealth is not enough. Far, far be it for me to interfere, but one or two little stratagems did occur to me..."

She couldn't help returning the old lady's impish smile.

"I'm all ears."

Two hours later, she pulled to a stop in front of Nakor's house. Armed for battle, she took a deep breath and marched towards the front door. It opened as soon as she approached, and Nakor strode over to meet her, as big and golden and gorgeous as ever. Her heart—and lower parts—did a frantic little flutter, and she realized this was going to be a very difficult war to win.

CHAPTER 17

A week later, Nakor was once again pacing his living room. The infuriating female was driving him slowly insane. She had invaded his home with fast food of all disgusting things and, even worse, gas station coffee, completely ignoring his protests. When he informed her that he wouldn't allow such a foul substance in his home, she'd had the nerve to cross her arms and tell him that if her coffee went, so would she.

She'd won that battle—but that didn't mean he'd given up. Twice he'd managed to slip a perfectly brewed espresso next to her while she was concentrating on her notes. He'd taken a great deal of delight in the blissful expression of pleasure on her face when she took a sip. And then she realized what he'd done.

"I told you I prefer my own coffee."

"That's impossible." He leaned down until their faces were only inches apart. "No matter how much you want to deny it, you know you enjoyed it."

Her little pink tongue flicked nervously across her lips before she lifted her chin and pushed the cup containing the remnants of the espresso towards him.

"I prefer my own."

Annoyed, he stalked away, but after she left that evening, he went to collect the cup and realized she'd finished it after all. He embarked on a campaign to make sure that she ate and drank actual food, leaving tempting little tidbits in places where she would be sure to find them. Several times he placed a softly steaming cup of Silver Needle next to his computer before making an excuse to leave. The level of tea in the cup was always lower when he returned.

His other main source of frustration was her clothing. The attractive outfits of the first few days had been replaced by baggy, oversized, torn clothing. Not only did it fail to make her any less attractive, he had to constantly fight the urge to rip them off of her and replace them with items that suited her beauty. Not to mention the fact that those teasing little glimpses of her pale skin through the holes—*holes!*—had kept him constantly erect.

Unfortunately, his offer to buy her a new wardrobe had not gone over well. If only she would let him care for her properly. He sighed and stalked out onto the deck.

His attempt to find a suitable present had also not been successful. She hadn't been impressed by rare orchids or handwoven silk scarves. She'd glared at him when he tried to give her a pretty little Cartier watch, a mere bauble really. A perfectly matched set of first edition Wilde had drawn a flicker of interest before she firmly shook her head. He'd even tried an extraordinarily well-balanced set of custom knives, but she'd looked amused rather than impressed when she refused them.

Despite the incredibly annoying week, a few things had gone well. He had managed to channel a lot of his frustration into his work and he'd made significant progress on the book. And she had continued to show up to work with him every day, her sweet scent filling his house, her laughter—when she forgot her anger—making his heart lighter. He couldn't imagine his life without her in it, but he was no closer to coming up with a plan to keep her than he'd been a week ago.

"I'm leaving," she announced from behind him, and he whirled around.

"What? Why? The sun has not yet begun to set."

She sighed, the collar of her oversized paint-splattered sweat-shirt slipping down to reveal her delicate collar bone. Even that brief hint of flesh sent a bolt of heat straight to his cock.

"We've been working every day for the past seven days. I need a break. Besides, there's a fall carnival in town today. I thought it might be fun to go."

She paused and he frowned at her.

"It will be crowded. And noisy. They will be selling abominations like funnel cakes and boiled peanuts."

"I like funnel cakes and boiled peanuts. I will enjoy going to the carnival."

He had the distinct feeling she was trying to tell him something, but he wasn't sure exactly what.

"You would be happier remaining here."

"No, I will be happier going to the carnival."

She would? It seemed inconceivable, but if that was truly what she wanted...

"Would you allow me to accompany you?"

Her smile was radiant enough to ignite both his heart and his cock.

"That would be very nice. Thank you for asking." She shot him a teasing glance from under her lashes. "I'll even go back to the inn and change in honor of the occasion."

"Would you like me to bring you an outfit?" he asked quickly, and she sighed.

"Don't ruin it, Nakor. Meet me at the inn in an hour."

He bit back a protest and nodded. He'd never been more thankful to have kept his mouth shut than when she greeted him at the door of the inn.

Her dark hair was in a loose braid over her shoulder, her eyes sparkling behind her glasses. She was wearing a frivolous fuzzy pink sweater that clung lovingly to her slight curves and a short, flirty black skirt with black tights and soft ankle boots. After a week of seeing her in nothing but oversized garments, she looked practically naked and his cock punched painfully against his jeans. He'd done his best to "dress down" in designer jeans and a handknit Irish wool sweater.

"You look beautiful. But then you always do," he added truthfully. "Even in those disgusting outfits you've been wearing."

Her mouth tightened for a moment, then she shook her head, muttering something about a leopard and spots, before her eyes drifted down over him.

"You look very nice as well."

He preened under her admiration, then pulled a small package out of his pocket.

"I brought you something. A very small something. Just because it's—" Rare? Expensive?—"Pretty," he said finally.

It was the right thing to say. She beamed at him as she took the pink knitted hat, and he carefully refrained from telling her it was knit from hand-dyed vicuna wool.

"This is perfect. It even matches my sweater."

"It is the color that tints your cheeks when you are pleased. Like now."

She looked up at him, her eyes wide and startled, and he couldn't resist stepping closer.

"May I kiss you?"

Her eyes dropped to his lips, and she nodded, almost shyly. He captured her face in his hands, marveling again at the silky texture of her skin, and kissed her. Somehow he managed to ignore the need that had been building for the past week and keep the kiss gentle, even as the soft sweetness of her mouth sent arousal flaming through his body. When he finally ended the kiss, her eyes were soft and dreamy. And curious.

"That was very restrained."

Did she sound disappointed?

"I am trying to behave," he growled.

"Hmm. Maybe if you can keep it up all evening, you can be a little less... restrained later."

She turned and walked away, her ass swaying in the provocative little skirt, and he had to recite the numbers of his Cayman bank accounts twice before he managed to wrest enough control over himself not to carry her back to his cave—*house*—immediately.

As soon as he did, he strode after her and tucked her small hand firmly in his arm. She gave him an impish look, but she didn't comment and they walked in silence except for their feet crunching in the fallen leaves. The sun was sinking over the river, setting fire to the autumn colors beginning to cover the trees covering the slope on the far side. He caught the scent of wood smoke and the distant hint of snow from the mountain peaks, as well as the teasing sweetness of her arousal.

Later, he told himself firmly as they turned on Elm Street.

As they drew closer to the town square, she looked up at him, her nose wrinkling adorably.

"The carnival smells wonderful."

"Of grease and sweat and dirt?" he asked dryly.

"Of happiness." She shook her head at him. "You have no soul."

"I assure you that I do—I am here, am I not?"

She tilted her head. "Why did you offer to come with me?"

"Because you said it would make you happy. And I intend to make you very, very happy, sweetheart."

This time, she was the one to stop and stare up at him, before he laughed and urged her on towards the carnival.

CHAPTER 18

*H*appiness fizzed through Charlotte's veins as they entered the bustling town square. Nakor had finally listened to what she really wanted—instead of what he thought she wanted. There had been several times over the past week when she'd wondered if the knowledge would make it through his thick skull before she punched him in the face—or pushed him to the ground and had her wicked way with him.

Of the two, the second seemed more likely, especially when their night together kept replaying in her head in glorious technicolor detail. But Flora had helped keep her strong, convincing her that it was in Nakor's best interests as well as hers, and providing her with ever more decrepit outfits.

Although she had started strategically enlarging some of the existing holes herself once she saw how riveted he was by those tiny hints of skin. It seemed only fair that he should suffer too.

Hopefully tonight neither one of them would be suffering.

The sun had disappeared behind the mountains by the time they reached the carnival, but the whole area was lit with hundreds of glowing Chinese lanterns. Colorful natural decorations surrounded the stalls lining the edges of the square—pine garlands, sprays of vibrant leaves, and heap upon heap of pumpkins and gourds and other autumn produce. There was a small stage with a dance floor in front of the Town Hall, and a row of rides along the riverfront.

People were wandering around everywhere, talking and laughing, and the fact that those people included werewolves and dryads and orcs didn't change the joyous smalltown atmosphere at all. She was surprised at how many people she already recognized. She caught a glimpse of Nichola's orange hair over by the craft beer tent, and saw Flora deep in conversation with another old lady, a witch's hat perched on top of her silver curls, while a distinguished older gentleman watched them from afar. Was that the mysterious Gladys?

A minotaur stomped over to join them, and she recognized him too. He was the one who had come over to speak to Nakor during their dinner.

"I have a quick question about—"

Nakor shook his head, interrupting the deep, booming voice.

"Not tonight, Mayor. We are here because my... female wishes to enjoy the carnival."

"Yes, of course. My apologies." The mayor shot her a quick look. "You're staying at the Fairhaven Falls Inn?"

Why did she want to blush? She really was staying there.

"I am. It's very nice."

"So I've heard." He tossed his head, the ring in his ear tinkling. "Have you, err, met any of the other guests?"

"A few. Several people have been in and out since I came."

"Hmm. Perhaps I should make sure Flora knows to tell her guests that they are welcome at the carnival. Pleased to meet you, ma'am." He nodded decisively and stomped away, an imposing figure even amongst the crowd of large Other males.

"Was it just me or was that odd?" she asked.

Nakor shook his head as he followed her gaze.

"It wasn't just you. I suspect that this time, Houston is the one with the problem. Now come on. You mentioned something about funnel cakes, and I would prefer to get that horror over with as soon as possible."

She laughed at his exaggerated shudder and followed him into the crowd.

For the next half-hour, she ate more fried junk food than she had in the last year. Nakor trailed after her with a long-suffering air, but he was clearly enjoying himself.

Several stalls had been set up with carnival style games, and they paused next to a ring toss. The object of the game was to toss a ring over a glass bowl containing a brightly colored fish in order to win the fish. A big red-headed werewolf kept purchasing three rings and tossing them over the bowls with unerring accuracy.

Each time the rings landed, the crowd of watching children would cheer, grab the bowls, and race over to the wall along the river with them.

"Why are they putting the bowls there—"

Before Nakor could answer her, three tentacles rose up out of the river, grabbed the bowls, and disappeared again.

Nakor shook his head, smiling, as she stared at the now smooth water.

"I'm not sure if Aiden is being quixotic or Sam is in search of an evening snack."

She decided she didn't want to know.

After her second funnel cake, they wandered through a long tent containing displays of local food and produce. Nakor stopped in front of a local farmer displaying a variety of charcuterie.

"Farmer Mac supplies Midnight Manor. His products are quite acceptable."

The farmer, a tall brown-skinned male with oddly furrowed skin, raised an eyebrow at the comment, but offered her several samples of his cured meats.

"These are delicious," she said enthusiastically, and the farmer smiled at her.

"It's a better choice than funnel cakes anyway," Nakor muttered as he bought a container of pate.

He also added a freshly made sourdough loaf, a jar of cranberry jelly, and a bottle of craft cider and carried their purchases to a bench next to the river. He insisted on feeding her even though she swore she wasn't hungry, and perhaps it was because of the crisp fall air, but she enjoyed every bite.

A surprising number of the people who walked by while they ate greeted him, and he responded cordially enough.

"You're really blowing your recluse image," she said, regarding him thoughtfully.

"I grew up here. I've known many of these people my entire life." He turned the half-empty container of pate in his hands. "Young dragons are less territorial. It's not until we reach our twenties that we start to prefer being alone."

"Does it bother you? Being here tonight?"

Amber eyes focused on her for a moment before he shook his head.

"No. My dragon recognizes this as neutral territory." He sounded almost surprised. "But there are limits as to how often and how long I can be around others. With some exceptions," he added, reaching for her hand and lifting it to his mouth to trace a quick fiery pattern across the back.

A shiver of anticipation traveled down her spine as she turned back to their meal. Just as they finished, a burst of color exploded overhead, and she gasped happily.

"Fireworks! I love fireworks."

"I find them enjoyable as well, like dragon fire in the night."

She'd never seen smalltown fireworks—they were so much closer and more personal than the grand ones in the city. The scent of gunpowder drifted across the river as the crowd oohed and aahed even the smallest shower of color. Nakor reached over and took her hand, but when she looked at him, his gaze was focused on the sky, his face filled with delight.

Afterwards she persuaded him to ride the carousel with her.

"This is a child's amusement," he protested, but she only grinned at him.

"I used to love riding the carousel in Central Park when I was a little girl. It's very romantic."

"Romantic?" He arched an eyebrow at her, then shook his head. "I can think of far more... romantic activities. But if you insist."

As soon as they stepped onto the platform, he scanned the available options.

"No dragons. How disappointing."

He decided on a golden lion instead, picking her up and depositing her on its back before swinging himself up behind her. He wrapped his arms around her, sliding his hands beneath the hem of her fuzzy little sweater, and she wiggled happily.

"Comfortable?" he asked, and she nodded, feeling ridiculously aroused, but also safe and secure and wonderfully warm.

"Perfectly."

He growled softly in response, the vibrations shooting through her body, as they moved up and down in time to the tinny music while the night spun around them. By the time the carousel slowly came to a stop, she was floating on a cloud of pink-tinged need. When he used the distraction created by the end of the ride to slip his hand higher beneath her sweater, tweaking a taut little peak, she almost exploded on the spot.

As they walked away from the carousel, more music caught her attention and she decided there was one more thing she wanted to do.

"Dance with me."

"Here?" She could tell he was going to refuse, but then he stopped and studied her face. "Is this what you want?"

She nodded, and they joined the couples circling the dance floor. He danced with the same powerful grace that marked all of his movements, and her arousal continued to build. She suddenly understood what he meant by a moment when the crowd became too much. She wanted to be alone with him. Now.

Her feet stopped moving even before the song ended, and he quickly whirled her out of the path of the oncoming couples.

"Is something wrong?"

"No. Something is right. Take me home, Nakor."

CHAPTER 19

By the time they made it back to Nakor's house, every muscle in his body was quivering from the strain of trying to hold himself in check. Charlotte seemed just as eager, her face flushed, her nipples stiff little peaks beneath her fuzzy sweater. His need was so strong it almost frightened him, and as soon as he had her safely inside his cave—*house*—he muttered an apology and stalked out on the balcony.

Throwing his head back, he breathed a stream of fire into the brilliant starlit night.

A satisfying quantity of gold and red sparks plumed into the heavens before he took a deep breath of cold night air and went back inside. She was standing at the windows, a bemused expression on her face.

"More fireworks," she said softly.

"Of a kind. I am a dragon, after all."

"I had noticed."

Then she smiled and came to join him, her face glowing. He lifted her into his arms, her delicious softness sending all of the blood in his body rushing to his cock.

"Now where were we?"

"I believe we were on our way to the bedroom," she murmured before nibbling on his ear. "Although I'm not fussy about location."

"If you keep that up, we won't make it another step." he groaned as her tongue teased at his ear. "And I have plans."

As soon as they entered the bedroom, he let her slide to the ground.

"Now take that ridiculous sweater off."

She giggled.

"I thought you liked my pink sweater."

"I like your lovely pink-tipped breasts much more."

She yanked the sweater over her head as he quickly stripped off his own clothes, his cock immediately thrusting towards her like a compass seeking true north. She was naked beneath the sweater, but it wasn't enough. He needed to see all of her. The rest of her clothes disappeared in an urgent rush before he swept her up in his arms and carried her to the bed, trying to control the need coursing through his veins.

The brief relief of his fire had already vanished, but he paused and looked down at her face as he gently removed her glasses.

"I've missed you, sweetheart," he whispered.

"I've missed you too."

"Then why—" He stopped and shook his head. He knew why. He couldn't even say she'd been wrong.

Her fingers brushed across his lips.

"Let's not talk about it now, Nakor. Let's just be together."

"Together. That's all I want."

He dipped his head and claimed her lips with his own. Her soft little cry echoed around his heart as he gave himself up to the glorious taste and feel of her. He took a deep breath of her sweet, familiar scent, tightening his already painfully hard cock further, but he ignored it as he kissed her. She tasted so good. So sweet. So perfect.

His mouth slid lower, stopping to tug a peaked nipple into his mouth and savor her gasp of pleasure. He continued to work the two stiff little points as his hand dipped between her thighs and found her slick and ready.

He pushed himself up against the head of the bed, then urged her on top of him.

"Straddle me, sweetheart."

A flush traveled down over her pretty breasts as she obeyed, stopping with her knees on either side of his hips, her soft little ass tormenting his aching cock.

"Is this what you wanted?"

"Perfect. Now lift up over me. Like this."

His hands went to her hips, and they both groaned as her hot, silken entrance kissed the tip of his cock. He let her set the pace, inching her way down, her breath catching at the stretch as she took his thick shaft deeper into her tight little channel.

The exquisite torment seemed to last forever before she released a final deep breath and took him completely. His control threatened to vanish when she moved tentatively, her sheath gripping him in a silken fist.

"You're so tight," he groaned as his hands went to her waist.

She started rocking against him, working her hips up and down his length as she leaned back into his hands. His tail coiled around her, holding her in place as his hips began to move, thrusting up into her as she quivered around him. He slid a hand between their bodies and found the hot little nub of her clit. As soon as he touched it she cried out, and then she was coming in long shuddering waves as his own climax swept over him, molten seed erupting into her perfect little body until she collapsed against him with another soft cry.

He cupped the back of her head with one hand and pressed her cheek against his chest as his tail curved up over her shoulders, stroking her gently.

"Mmm," she said after a long silence. "Is that how dragons mate? With each other, I mean."

"Sometimes."

She immediately picked up on the fact that he was being evasive and looked up at him, her eyes narrowed.

"And other times?"

"Other times in midair," he admitted reluctantly. "Mating flights are traditional amongst our people."

As he feared, her eyes widened in distress.

"But I can't fly."

"It's of no consequence. I would rather have you in my bed than a thousand females in midair."

She gave a somewhat watery giggle.

"A thousand does sound excessive."

He hesitated, his fingers playing with the soft strands of her hair. He didn't want to upset her, but he had given the matter considerable thought during the past week and there was another possibility...

"If you ever... wished to take a mating flight with me, I would be delighted to carry you."

Her pretty little teeth clamped down on her lower lip.

"I'm not sure that I could do that. Heights aren't my favorite thing."

"And that's absolutely fine. I just wanted you to know. In case you ever wished to... explore."

He couldn't read the thoughts behind those big grey eyes, but then she gave him a seductive smile.

"There are other things I wish to explore right now."

CHAPTER 20

*N*akor helped Charlotte explore so thoroughly that she drifted off to sleep once he finally slipped free. The next time she opened her eyes, he was staring down at her.

"What?" she mumbled sleepily.

"I've been waiting for you to wake up. Come with me," he demanded, then lifted her into his arms without waiting for her to agree.

She squeaked and put her arms around his neck.

"Can't I even get dressed first?"

"Clothing is a human custom."

"And I'm human, in case you hadn't noticed."

He looked down at her, his eyes glittering.

"Oh, I noticed. And I can appreciate it even more when you are unclothed."

"At least give me my glasses."

When he obeyed, she stopped arguing.

He carried her through the bedroom and into an enormous walk-in closet lined with impeccably neat clothes. Before she could do more than give him a puzzled look, he pushed a hidden button next to the full-length mirror. The mirror slid aside to reveal a set of stone steps leading down. The steps were as sleek and expensive as everything else in his house, but the passageway still had an oddly primitive feel as they wound down the steps.

The stairs ended on a cool, dim floor with a glass-doored wine cave at one end.

"Did you bring me here for a drink?" she asked dryly, and he gently nipped her nose.

"Hush, female."

He pressed another concealed device, and this time one of the stone walls slid silently to one side and she gasped in amazement. A glittering treasure trove waited on the other side of the wall. An enormous collection of jewelry was displayed across multiple glass shelves, along with many other small, valuable items—everything from ancient figurines to jeweled snuff boxes to tiny miniatures in ornate frames. The only common denominator seemed to be that everything sparkled or gleamed in the overhead lights. An enormous heap of gold coins was piled in one corner, and from the way it was formed, she suspected that he had sat there many times.

"Oh my God. Is this your hoard?"

"Yes—I mean, no. A modern dragon does not have a hoard. This is my storage locker."

"If you say so."

"It is only in case of emergency," he added. "My true hoard, my wealth, is in a bank. Well, banks."

He put her down as he talked and started retrieving various items from the shelves, holding them up against her before moving on. When he started adorning her with various pieces, she began to object, then decided it was more as if he were playing dress up than trying to impress her with his wealth.

"Why did you start writing?" she asked as he strung three jeweled chains around her waist.

"I'm not entirely sure." He shrugged. "I wasn't interested in acquiring any more companies, and although my grandfather would roll over in his grave if he heard me say it, you can only spend so much time admiring your hoard."

A delicate crown dripping with sapphires was placed on her head.

"I think the writing was a way to explore some of my other interests."

"They're still about treasure," she pointed out as he stacked bracelets up her arms.

"True."

"But I also think it's more than that. Your books are a way to communicate. And maybe you needed that as your dragon became more isolated."

A pendant settled between her breasts, a huge oval diamond in a filigreed pearl setting. He fingered the edge of it for a moment, the feel of his fingers against her skin awakening her still simmering arousal.

"You could be right. Does it matter?"

"Not really. I just like knowing what makes you tick."

Amber eyes glowed down at her.

"You do." To her shock, he started removing the jewelry, stripping it off even more rapidly than he'd put it on. "You don't need any of this. You are perfect exactly the way you are."

Her throat threatened to close but she managed a smile.

He waited until all the jewelry was gone, until she was naked once more, then drew her into his arms.

"I love you, Charlotte. I never want to lose you again."

"I love you too."

This time, she couldn't hold back the tears, but they didn't matter because he was kissing her and loving her and carrying her back to bed, leaving his hoard unlocked and forgotten behind him.

THE NEXT WEEK PASSED IN A DAZE OF HAPPINESS, WITH one small exception—they never discussed the future. They seemed to have reached an unspoken agreement to put that conversation on hold until the book was finished.

Other than that one detail, everything was perfect. They laughed and loved—and argued. He still had a tendency to slip into his arrogant, materialistic ways but at least he listened to her—even if sometimes she had to grab him by the cock to force him to pay attention. He taught her about tea, and she taught him about macaroni and cheese. He wrote, and she did some additional research, although it was for another potential book now—another subject they had put on hold.

After the second night with him, she decided there was no point in pretending she was going to return to the inn and told Flora she was moving out. The old lady just grinned at her.

"You actually held out longer than I expected. Just as well the two of you worked things out. I have another woman coming next week."

"Umm, okay?"

"One more decision to go," Flora said, her eyes twinkling. "But I know you'll make the right one."

"Cryptic much?" she sighed to Alison after Flora disappeared with her usual speed.

"I think that's her specialty. Along with mysterious entrances. Oh, and matchmaking, of course."

"Matchmaking?"

Alison grinned as she pulled a tray of cookies out of the oven. "I'm firmly convinced that Flora intends to pair off everyone in town before she dies."

She was thinking about that conversation now as she brewed two cups of espresso and carried them out onto the deck. Nakor was watching the sunrise as usual, and she'd grown familiar enough with his routine to carry the cup over to him at the railing. It was fine—as long as she didn't look down. His tail curved around her waist as he took his cup.

"You know the book is ready to go to the editor," she said quietly.

His wings fluttered, but he didn't respond.

"I thought I'd take it to New York with me."

"Don't go."

The words were almost inaudible over the agitated flapping of his wings.

"I have to go. It's my job."

"I'll buy you another publishing company. Hell, I think I already own one."

"That's not the answer and you know it."

"Is that what you want?" The words sounded as if they were torn out of him. "What will make you happy?"

You will.

But she didn't say it out loud. Not yet. At some point during the previous week, she'd realized that she needed to return to the city. To see if she was ready to replace the dream she'd held for so long with a new dream.

"I want—I need—to go back to the city," she said softly. "Just to see."

"I understand."

She didn't think he did, but there was nothing more she could do about it right now.

"When are you leaving?" he added.

"Today. Delaying it would only make it worse." And weaken her resolve. "Will you take me to the airport?"

"I can't. There is no way I would ever allow you to get on that plane."

The flare of his old arrogance was oddly reassuring.

"All right. I'll make other arrangements."

He didn't respond, and he didn't look at her.

"I love you, Nakor."

At that he threw up his head, eyes blazing.

"I love you too, which is the only reason I'm still standing here instead of locking you in my hoard where you belong. So if you want to leave, you'd better leave now."

Oh. She was really tempted to forget her decision and succumb to all that banked passion. Instead, she gave a quick nod and hurried away, forcing back the tears. As she did, she heard an agonized cry and saw the plume of fire shooting into the sky behind her.

Two days later, Charlotte stepped out of Bird Publishing for the last time. Marjorie hadn't been thrilled with her departure, but her gratitude over receiving the manuscript had helped soften her harsh tongue. It probably hadn't hurt that there were rumors of another round of budget cuts in the new year.

In the end, it hadn't been such a hard decision after all. The people, the company, she'd loved were gone. Even publishing itself had changed radically over the past seven years. She still wanted to go back to helping authors, but it would be through a new forum.

She glanced up the street to look for a cab and her heart skipped a beat. A tall golden figure leaned against the building next door, impeccably clad in a bespoke Italian wool suit, his head down and his hands in his pockets. God, she'd missed him. She'd spent all night tossing and turning, missing his familiar warmth and the comforting presence of his arms and tail wrapped around her.

She didn't even hesitate—she walked straight into his arms, sighing with relief as they closed around her. The tension that had plagued her for the past two days vanished as she took in a deep breath of his comforting cinnamon scent. Then she smiled up into that beloved face.

"Hi there."

"Hello, sweetheart."

"I suppose you just happened to be in the neighborhood?"

"No, I came looking for you. After you left, I walked around the house in a daze. I think I even set a few things on fire. Then I decided I was being foolish. I can always build a new cave. If you want to live here, we'll live here."

Her heart fluttered.

"You'd hate it here."

"If the cave is high enough and isolated enough, I can adapt."

"God, I love you."

His eyes glittered as he stroked her cheek.

"And that's why I'm here."

"It means so much to me that you came." She smiled up at him. "Now let's go home. Back to Fairhaven Falls."

"Are you sure?"

"Positive. I just handed in my notice. It's a little short, but then she has the next Nakor Earlsworth bestseller in her hands. She was thrilled about the sexy librarian joining Griff's adventures. Honestly, I think she was more interested in using that to bring in new readers than my departure. I'm all yours."

A slightly smoky sigh escaped him.

"Thank the gods."

"I will have to do something about selling my apartment. I would suggest keeping it in case we wanted to visit, but I'm not sure you'd even make it through the door."

"I have a real estate firm on retainer," he assured her as he guided her quickly towards a waiting limo.

"Of course you do," she murmured, but she squeezed his hand as he helped her inside.

"Airport," he ordered the driver, then closed the partition and settled back against the seat, pulling her into his arms with another long sigh.

"Don't we have to book a flight first?" she asked as she snuggled against him.

"No, I brought my jet." He suddenly gave her a horrified look. "You aren't going to try and make me take a commercial airline to prove a point, are you? Because I may have given in to funnel cakes and macaroni and cheese, but I am not flying commercial. Ever."

"Never?" she asked teasingly, slipping her hand under his jacket to the superfine cotton shirt below.

"You know, sweetheart, two people can play that game." His hand slid up under her skirt, landing unerringly over her clit. "And my jet has a nice big bedroom. I have every intention of making love to you all the way home."

"I'm convinced," she gasped, as he applied the perfect amount of pressure.

She just hoped she could make it to the plane.

EPILOGUE

 *ix weeks later...*

"Almost finished?" Nakor demanded as he joined Charlotte in the study.

"Yes. Unless you want me to tidy up first?"

She hid a smile when he slowly shook his head, even though it clearly pained him to do so. Her desk was littered with plans and budgets and the astonishing variety of paperwork required by her new project. It turned out that he did in fact own a now defunct publishing house, and she was determined to resurrect it in a new version, one designed to work with small, independent authors.

Normally she tried to at least clear the surface when she finished for the day, but time had slipped away from her so she left everything where it was as she went to change.

"Are you sure about this?" she asked a short time later.

"Of course," he replied immediately and she rolled her eyes.

"Why did I even bother asking? You're always sure."

"That is because I am always right. Almost always," he amended when she raised an eyebrow. "You have proven to be correct once or twice."

"You know, I really don't think you're helping yourself here."

He grinned and snatched her up into his arms, kissing her until she was breathless, then smiling down into her dazed face.

"I know I was right when I asked you to be my mate. Nothing else really matters."

He could be so sweet when he wanted to be. She sighed and took his hand, letting him lead her out to the parking area in front of the house. He always took off from one of the decks when he flew alone, but they had discovered during their practice flights that she had an easier time if they started from a nice, flat surface.

"Are you ready?" he asked, once they were in the center of the area.

"I suppose."

He gently lifted her chin.

"We really don't have to do this now. Or ever. I love you and you love me. That is all that really matters."

"I know. But I want to—and we have been practicing." She managed a shaky but sincere smile. "Plus it would be a shame to waste that outfit."

His scales rippled as he preened for her, but his pride was completely justified. He had donned a type of kilt made of thin, flexible strips of gold that revealed teasing glimpses of thick muscled thighs—not to mention the heavy weight of his cock. The wide belt around his waist was studded with cabochon rubies the size of robin's eggs. Matching cuffs circled his wrists, a ceremonial necklace glittered on his chest, and a gold and ruby circlet rested beneath his horns.

After an extensive debate about her garment, they had agreed on a short Grecian style toga fastened with gold ribbons. She too wore rubies—much more modest ones—in a simple pendant and bracelet combination.

He smoothed a hand down over his kilt and nodded.

"You're right. It would be a shame to waste it."

She nodded, then took a deep breath as he swung her up into his arms.

"Hold on tight," he warned, his wings already spreading behind him.

A moment later she felt them flex, and they were airborne.

The late fall afternoon was cold and clear, but the heat radiating off his body kept her comfortably warm as he circled slowly over the town. They had come this far before—once, briefly—and there was something reassuring in the familiar sights. He started to climb again and she closed her eyes until he leveled back out.

"You can open your eyes now, sweetheart."

She did and gave a little cry of amazement. They were above the clouds now, and the mountains rose up around them, their peaks shrouded in snow. The sun was setting to the west, the sky darkening to the east.

"It's beautiful."

"More beautiful now that you're here."

She turned her head away from the magnificent surroundings and met his glowing amber eyes. He studied her face for a moment, then one hand left her as he began to release the ribbons on her dress. She still felt perfectly safe, secure in the strength of his other arm, his tail supporting her butt. He worked quickly and soon she was bare except for the jewels.

His magnificent cock had emerged from its sheath, pushing free of his kilt, and she traced the spiraling ridge with her fingers as he groaned. He urged her back over his arm, making sure she felt secure as he bent to take a diamond hard peak in his mouth. The shocking wet heat of his mouth sent a bolt of electricity through her system, and she arched against his mouth, forgetting everything except that hot, demanding pull.

His mouth worked each peak in turn as his hand slipped beneath her to strum her aching clit. Her entire body quivered on the verge of climax when he shifted her, positioning her directly over his massive cock. He held her there, paused for a moment, his eyes meeting hers, then slowly lowered her inch by excruciating inch on to his broad shaft.

She groaned as the thick ridge spiraled into her channel, adding another layer of sensation to the overwhelming pressure. Once he had filled her completely, he held her there, his tail preventing her from moving even an inch.

"Do you know how good you feel? How incredible it feels to have your tight little cunt wrapped around me like this?"

His voice was deeper, rougher than she had ever heard it, and she tried to wiggle on his cock. He refused to allow her to move, his tail holding her in place as he claimed her lips with his. He took his time, tasting every bit of her mouth, stroking the insides with his tongue.

And then he began to fly, his wings flaring behind him as he lifted her up and down his cock while they swooped and soared across the sky. She clutched at his shoulders as they shot higher and higher, her body lost to a terrifying ecstasy.

These were not the calm easy glides of their practice flights. This was the primal glory of a mating dragon, and all she could do was surrender to him.

Nakor flew faster and faster, plunging harder and deeper into her body until she was perched on the precipice of climax, and then he abruptly rolled in mid-air and she screamed as her body went up in a firestorm of pleasure. He roared, throwing his head back as a fiery plume of red and gold sparks ignited overhead against the darkening sky.

Heat erupted inside her in a rush of exquisite agony, and she convulsed around him as wave after wave of unimaginable pleasure rushed through her body. Nothing else existed except the two of them and the endless expanse of the sky.

NAKOR WRAPPED HIMSELF AROUND HIS MATE AS FIRE ripped through his body, his cock pulsing helplessly in the rhythm of his flight. He had never imagined the pleasure, the sheer ecstasy of a mating flight with the female he loved. Even though he never wanted it to end, his weary body eventually stopped pumping his seed into her welcoming depths. Keeping her locked firmly against his chest, his flight softened into a gentle guide.

She sagged against him, trusting that he would keep her safe and in its own way, that was almost as satisfying at the mating flight.

"Where are we going?" she eventually murmured in a sleepy voice.

"Home. I think you've earned a hot bath and a glass of champagne."

"I definitely earned it."

"Yes, you did."

He chuckled as he stroked over her abused little clit, and she squeaked and opened one eye.

"Closed for business."

"Indeed? For how long?"

"At least an hour."

"I think I can wait that long."

They were back home and he was carrying her into the bedroom before she opened her eyes again. He looked down to see her giving him a thoughtful look.

"Was that... all right?"

"All right?"

"I mean, because I'm not a dragon."

He pressed a quick kiss to the tiny furrow between her brows.

"It could not possibly have been any better. And the fact that you trusted me enough to fly with me... to mate with me... It means everything to me."

"I think saying I enjoyed it too wouldn't even scratch the surface. We should do it again."

It seemed his cock was not completely drained after all, jerking against her stomach as he laid her on the bed.

"As tempting as that prospect sounds, right now you need rest."

"Okay," she agreed sleepily.

But he couldn't bring himself to leave, and sat down next to her instead.

"Thank you, sweetheart," he said softly.

"Thank you? For what?"

"For coming to find me. For refusing to leave. For not giving up on me when I was an idiot. For loving me."

Her beautiful grey eyes sparkled with tears as she very carefully removed her glasses and set them aside. Then she smiled up at him and held out her hand.

"I guess I don't need an hour after all. Come here, my love."

He very happily obeyed.

AUTHOR'S NOTE

Thank you so much for reading ***Fireworks for My Dragon Boss***! I had so much fun spinning my own variation of a billionaire - dragon! - boss. Charlotte was the perfect person to show Nakor that there are more important things in life than material possessions - and of course I had fun playing with the writing elements! I hope you enjoyed the story as much as I did!

Whether you enjoyed the story or not, it would mean the world to me if you left an honest review on Amazon – reviews are one of the best ways to help other readers find my books!

Thank you all for supporting these books - I couldn't do it without you!

And, as always, a special thanks to my beta team – Janet S, Nancy V, and Kitty S. Your thoughts and comments are incredibly helpful!

Coming up next - ***The Single Mom and the Orc***!

*Trogar likes his solitary life just fine - until
Pippa, a single mom on the run with a new baby, arrives in
Fairhaven Falls. With a little arm twisting from the ever helpful
Flora, Trogar soon finds himself enmeshed in their lives - and
loving every reluctant moment.*

*But can Trogar hammer his way into Pippa's heart before her
past catches up with her?*

The Single Mom and the Orc is available on Amazon!

Ready for another cozy monster romance? Then you'll love
Extra Virgin Gargoyle!

*When Angie accepts a part-time job cataloging the library of the
vast Gothic mansion on the edge of town, the brooding gargoyle
owner turns out to be even more fascinating than his collection.*

Can a curvy librarian tame a grumpy gargoyle?

Extra Virgin Gargoyle is available on Amazon!

To make sure you don't miss out on any new releases, please
visit my website and sign up for my newsletter!

www.honeyphillips.com

OTHER TITLES

COZY MONSTERS

Fairhaven Falls

Cupcakes for My Orc Enemy

Trouble for My Troll

Fireworks for My Dragon Boss

The Single Mom and the Orc

Monster Between the Sheets

Extra Virgin Gargoyle

Without a Stitch

HOMESTEAD WORLDS

Seven Brides for Seven Alien Brothers

Artek

Benjar

Callum

Drakkar

Endark

Frantor

Gilmat

You Got Alien Trouble!

Cosmic Fairy Tales

Jackie and the Giant

Blind Date with an Alien

Her Alien Farmhand

KAISARIAN EMPIRE

The Alien Abduction Series

Anna and the Alien

Beth and the Barbarian

Cam and the Conqueror

Deb and the Demon

Ella and the Emperor

Faith and the Fighter

Greta and the Gargoyle

Hanna and the Hitman

Izzie and the Icebeast

Joan and the Juggernaut

Kate and the Kraken

Lily and the Lion

Mary and the Minotaur

Nancy and the Naga

Olivia and the Orc

Exposed to the Elements

The Naked Alien

The Bare Essentials

A Nude Attitude

The Buff Beast

The Strip Down

The Alien Invasion Series

Alien Selection

Alien Conquest

Alien Prisoner

Alien Breeder

Alien Alliance

Alien Hope

Alien Castaway

Alien Chief

Alien Ruler

Horned Holidays

Krampus and the Crone

A Gift for Nicholas

A Kiss of Frost

Cyborgs on Mars

High Plains Cyborg

The Good, the Bad, and the Cyborg

A Fistful of Cyborg

A Few Cyborgs More

The Magnificent Cyborg

The Outlaw Cyborg

The Cyborg with No Name

ABOUT THE AUTHOR

Honey Phillips writes steamy science fiction stories about hot alien warriors and the human women they can't resist. From abductions to invasions, the ride might be rough, but the end always satisfies.

Honey wrote and illustrated her first book at the tender age of five. Her writing has improved since then. Her drawing skills, unfortunately, have not. She loves writing, reading, traveling, cooking, and drinking champagne - not necessarily in that order.

Honey loves to hear from her wonderful readers! You can stalk her at any of the following locations...

www.facebook.com/HoneyPhillipsAuthor
www.bookbub.com/authors/honey-phillips
www.instagram.com/HoneyPhillipsAuthor
www.honeyphillips.com

Printed in Great Britain
by Amazon

42488141R10098